Praise for

The Kindness Challenge

"Beautiful, thought-provoking . . . This inspiring tale of Christ-inspired love, told through a season of grief and Christmas joy, will make you pause and consider what your holiday season could look like."
—**Amanda Wright, 2025 Christy Award Winner**

"*The Kindness Challenge* is a feel-good Christmas story of hope and generosity in the face of loss. Though the characters are grieving a husband and father gone too soon, the acts of kindness performed in his name by his widow and children are a testament to the way our loved ones live on in our hearts. Melissa Cate has crafted an uplifting and emotional family story that inspires a spirit of Christian charity and drives home the true meaning of the holiday season."
—**Katie Fitzgerald, author of *All Year with Anthony* and *Coming Back to Christmas***
Winner of Spark Flash Fiction's 2025 Contest issue

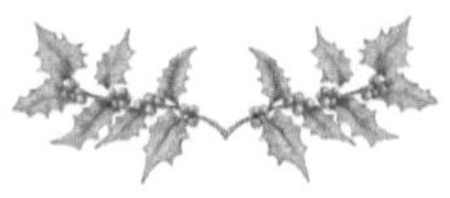

"This is a beautifully written story encompassing the heart of kindness and patience during a challenging time within a grieving family. *The Kindness Challenge* gives a heartfelt message about navigating through a holiday season with children as a now-widowed parent.
It gives hope and makes you smile at all the ways we can not only show kindness, but remember our loved ones in the small things while doing it.
Faith and love are woven into these pages flawlessly. A great short read that will warm your heart."
—Alyssa Feliciano, Christlit Award Winning Author

"I laughed at the silly jokes, got nostalgic with the whimsical stories, and cried with the family in their grief. Though the underlying subject matter is heavy, the story itself never is and is imbued with hope throughout. I absolutely adored the story and would recommend it to anyone looking for fresh new ideas to incorporate in to their holidays, those who are grieving losses, and to any who enjoy stories about family and/or Christmas."
—Erin Laramore, ARC Reader

The Kindness Challenge

A CHRISTMASTIME NOVELLA

MELISSA CATE

an imprint of Nicole Frail Books, LLC
Avoca, Pennsylvania

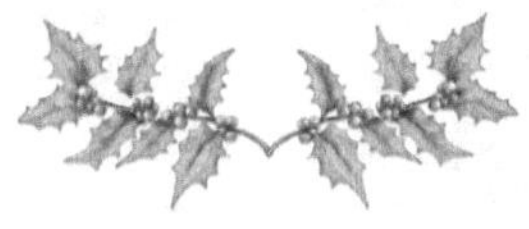

For Randee and the life we didn't get to have together.

"My Good Shepherd" by Randee Cate

"Then Jesus said, 'Come to me, all of you who are weary and
carry heavy burdens, and I will give you rest.'"
Matthew 11:28 (NLT)

Dear Reader,

Thank you for taking the time to read this very personal story. This was written shortly after my husband unexpectedly passed away and was a way of keeping a bit of him close to us as we approached Christmas.

While the story is fictional, you'll find nods to him and our life together throughout the story. Besides the ones I'm sharing here, there are a number of other hints at who he was to us. Those who knew him well will find him in the pages.

One of the traditions we have had since our daughter was a preschooler is having Christmas angels visit who challenge the kids to acts of kindness every day of December leading up to Christmas, thus our "Kindness Challenge."

My husband's first initial was "R," and he sometimes used "Ark8" when sharing some of his artwork. He was a brilliant artist in every medium he tried. I never ceased to be amazed at what he could come up with. The artwork shared at the end of this book is one of his hand-drawn pieces.

Apple fritters were his favorite donuts. Chicken fajitas with pineapple-mango salsa was the first meal he ever made for me. His favorite Christmas movie really was *A Christmas Story*. He loved making pancakes for our kids, and our daughter enjoyed having "drawing contests" with him.

Ultimately, our hope is in Jesus, and we know where my husband is now. That hope is what allows me to share *The Kindness Challenge* with you now. My hope is that it will encourage you to find your own ways to include a loved one who might not be with you—for whatever reason—during a time of celebration.

With Love,

Melissa Cate

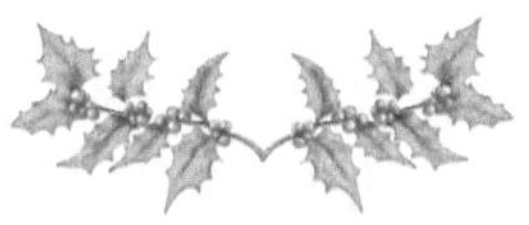

THE SMELLS OF THE DAY before still lingered. Pumpkin, cinnamon, cranberry, turkey. They mingled in the air, and Leah drew a deep breath, savoring the comfort they brought. She sat alone at the breakfast nook, her fingers wrapped around a mug of coffee. Tears sprung to her eyes as she glimpsed the book lying open on the table.

In a few days, she would continue a tradition her children enjoyed every December. Twenty-five days of kindness. Sometimes random. Sometimes not so random. A daily note challenging them to a specific act of kindness. She thought of Jacob's neat printing of the notes in years past. She sighed as she pictured him, quietly sealing an envelope and tucking it into the picture frame that hung between their bedrooms for them to find the next morning. This year had to look different, even if her little loves didn't understand that. Even if she didn't know how just yet.

She drew the mug to her mouth, sipping at the energy-giving liquid and hoping it would provide her brain with a jolt. Closing her eyes, she murmured a quick prayer for wisdom. She blinked as memories flashed in her mind and began making notes in her book, coffee forgotten as ideas began to take shape—ways for her and the kids to feel like her husband was home for the holidays.

December 1

LEAH SMILED AS HER CHILDREN walked into Ark8 Design, carrying boxes from the local bakery. She spied the receptionist, Brenda, who finished a phone call before greeting them.

"Hi, Lucy! Hi, Micah! What brings y'all in today?" Brenda walked around her desk. "I'm so glad to see you three," she whispered as she hugged Leah.

"We brought Daddy's favorite donuts to share with everyone." Despite her matter-of-fact response, tears sprung in Lucy's eyes as she bit her lip.

"That was mighty nice of you, sweetheart. Would you like to take them to the offices, or would you like to put them in the breakroom?"

Nine-year-old Micah shrugged as he looked at his sister. Lucy's eyes widened as she glanced at Leah to answer.

"I think they'd like to visit a couple of offices, but leave the rest," answered Leah. Lucy nodded in agreement with her mother.

Brenda's gaze softened. "Certainly. You know where everyone is."

"Thank you." Leah started toward the back, turning when she noticed Micah hadn't followed.

Micah tilted his head toward Brenda, and Leah grinned. "Would you like an apple fritter, Brenda?" Micah asked.

"I'd love one, thank you." She helped Micah with the box and set a fritter on her desk before kneeling down to his level. "This was very sweet of you, Micah."

Micah blushed and hurried off after his mom.

Leah ambled to the back offices and knocked on a door before poking her head inside. "Hey, Chris."

Surprise flickered over Chris's face as he looked up and smiled. "Leah!" He stood and walked around his desk. Micah peeked out from behind Leah, while Lucy stepped up beside her. "Lucy and Micah, too! It's so nice to see you." He gave Leah a brief hug before stepping back.

"Lucy and Micah brought donuts for everyone."

Leah slid her hand along Lucy's back, offering her silent support. The tween's anxiety had increased since Jacob's death, but she was fighting it every day.

"That's so kind of you two! Thank you." He turned to the chairs in his office. "Come, have a seat for a moment."

The trio walked in. Micah's eyes grew bigger as he eyed a crate of toys in the corner. He handed the box of donuts to Leah and made his way to the toys.

"Wait, Micah. Those aren't for you."

Micah's head drooped and he started back toward a chair. Chris stopped him. "It's okay, Micah. You're welcome to play with those. I have them for when Scarlett needs to come to work with me."

Micah grinned, brought his hand to his chin, and extended it out and down toward Chris.

"You're welcome," Chris replied.

Leah leaned toward Chris and whispered, "He's been pretty quiet since Jacob died. He talks more at home, but out and about, he uses some signs that he learned at school. He's getting there. Counseling is helping."

"I think he just misses Daddy," piped in Lucy from beside Leah.

Chris nodded at Lucy. "I bet you're right." He dropped his voice to a whisper. "I think we all do."

Lucy rubbed her hands together to soothe her heart and nodded. A tear escaped and she brushed it away with the back of her hand.

December 2

Dear Lucy and Micah,

I'm so proud of you. You did a great job handing out apple fritters yesterday. Your daddy was a great artist. Today, I would like for you to each make at least two pictures for us to take to some of the seniors in our neighborhood. We'll deliver them later this week.

Love,

Mama

LUCY'S TONGUE STUCK OUT OF the side of her mouth as she concentrated on her second drawing. Micah had finished and was eating some Goldfish. He bent over Lucy to look at her picture.

"Micah! You got crumbs on my picture!" The tween burst into tears as she yelled for her mom.

"I'm sorry! I just wanted to see it!" Micah erupted in tears.

Leah walked in and hugged the youngsters. They

collapsed into a heap on the floor, hugging and crying together. Lucy leaned against her mom, burying her face in Leah's shoulder. Micah knelt next to them, his arms stretched over their shoulders. Leah smoothed Lucy's hair as she sobbed. Their weight against her was a stark reminder of all the things she now carried alone, and fresh tears sprung to her eyes.

"I miss our drawing contests," wailed Lucy, sitting back and wiping away the tears streaming down her face.

"I know, sweetheart," whispered Leah, rubbing Lucy's back.

"I miss Daddy," cried Micah.

Leah pulled her son close. "Me, too, bubba, me, too."

Lucy sat up. "What do you miss most, Mama?"

Leah thought for a moment. "I miss a lot of things. One thing I miss most is how much he loved to make pancakes for you two."

Micah giggled. "They were funny."

"Yes," agreed Leah. "They could be."

"Where did Daddy learn to make pancakes like that?" asked Lucy.

Leah breathed deeply as she remembered Jacob's discovery of making pancake art. "Well, sweetheart, he saw a video once of someone else making pancakes shaped like different things. And he had to try it." The memories of Jacob having several bottles of different colored pancake batter were vivid in her mind. "Daddy was such a great artist that he could make a whole scene in one pancake." She tapped her daughter's nose. "He practiced *a lot* when you were a toddler and perfected the technique so he could make those awesome pancakes. He tested different recipes and mixes, trying to find the best-tasting one that he could design with."

"They were yummy." Lucy grinned. "Especially when he added pumpkin spice. My favorite."

"Do you remember when he made some I could build with?" asked Micah.

Leah nodded. "I do. *That* particular recipe he had to Google."

Micah's brow furrowed, and he leaned away from Leah. "Why?"

"Well, bubba, he knew you wouldn't be able to build something that stood with pancakes that were bendy and not able to hold much shape. He had to find a recipe that made them a little stronger, even if the taste wasn't quite the same."

Micah's jaw went slack. "That explains *so* much." He stared at Leah, unblinking, his mouth in a firm line. "They did *not* taste good at *all*."

Lucy started snickering. "Those pancakes were *not* pancakes."

Leah laughed with her. "No, they were not."

Micah folded his arms over his chest. "Someone could have told me that *before* I tried to eat them."

Leah bit her lip to stop laughing. "I'm sorry, Micah. He really just wanted to make you happy with something you could build with that was edible and looked like pancakes."

"Well—" Micah paused. "They definitely *looked* like pancakes. Taste is a different story." He chuckled.

"Mama?" asked Lucy.

"Yeah?"

"Could we have pancakes for dinner tonight?"

December 3

Dear Lucy and Micah,

I love how much care you put into the pictures you made for our neighbors. I'm sure they will be a hit. Today, let's give out candy canes as we do some grocery shopping and pick out gifts for your best friends. We'll give a candy cane to anyone who helps us in any way.

Love,
Mama

LUCY LOOKED UP AT THE highest shelf and grinned at Leah. "Mama, could we get some of that sauce up there?"

Leah raised an eyebrow as she followed Lily's finger. "Tzatziki sauce?" She paused. "I'm not sure I can reach it."

"Is that how you say it?" giggled Lucy.

"Have you had it before?" Leah was puzzled. Lucy wasn't her adventurous eater. That was Micah.

"No, but I think we should try it."

Lucy nodded toward the couple walking toward

them, and Leah noticed they were both taller than her. *They can probably reach the high shelf*, thought Leah.

She smiled at Lucy. "Sure thing, if we're able to get it without breaking it. We can use it for sheet pan chicken this week."

Lucy hurried up to the couple who had stopped to look at the variety of specialty cheese. "Excuse me, please?" When they turned, Lucy rushed through her request. "Would you please help us get some tza-tza-tza, well, some sauce from the top shelf? My mom and I are too short to reach it, and my brother is even smaller." She took a deep breath. "Whew."

The couple laughed as they followed Lucy to the sauce and got it down for her. As Lucy accepted the sauce, she handed them two candy canes. "Thank you for your help! I hope you like candy canes."

The woman smiled. "We do, thank you. We'll have them with our hot chocolate later. Happy to help."

As they walked off, Lucy turned to Leah. "That one was too easy." She looked at Micah, who quickly shook his head. "Bubba, come on! You need to help me! I can't ask everyone." He continued to shake his head.

Leah put her hand on Lucy's shoulder. "It's okay. He can pick out people for us to ask for help, and he can give out some of the candy canes."

Lucy let out a sigh. "Can you *at least* come up with an idea for the help we need?" She pointed back and forth between them. "It's supposed to be a team effort."

Leah pursed her lips to keep from interrupting. She wanted them to figure it out together—and if she was completely honest with herself, she was ready for Micah to start talking in public again. Maybe Lucy could persuade him.

Micah tugged on Lucy's coat sleeve, and she bent down. He whispered in her ear. She whispered back to him. He nodded and whispered in her ear some more. He stepped back.

"Mama?" asked Lucy.

"What's up?"

"Could we go to the pet aisle?"

"We aren't getting a pet right now."

"I know. Trust us. Micah has a great idea."

As they meandered to the pet aisle, they saw a teen-ager helping a senior citizen with some things they'd knocked from the shelves. When the aisle was orderly once again, Lucy ran over and handed them both a candy cane. "Merry Christmas!" she called as she hurried back to Leah and Micah.

"Nice, Lucy." Leah gave her daughter a side hug. "I love how you notice people and the nice things they do for each other."

Lucy blushed at the praise then turned to the dog toys. "Here we go. . . . Hmmm."

Micah also stared at the dog toys.

Leah raised her eyebrows as she observed them for a moment.

Lucy pointed at a fuzzy and squeaky toy. Micah shook his head and pointed at a giant bone. Lucy pointed at another toy. "Maybe this one?"

Micah pulled a toy off the shelf.

Leah was sure her face reflected her confusion. "Um—"

"Trust us!" came Lucy's stage whisper.

Leah continued to watch them. It was comical to see them silently disagree over toys for a dog they didn't even have.

Another shopper came down the aisle, and Leah moved out of the way as he stopped to grab a couple of toys from the hooks. Micah elbowed Lucy and tilted his head toward the man.

Lucy took a deep breath. "Excuse me, sir?" She put on her bravest face as the man turned toward her.

"Oh. I'm sorry. Let me move my cart," he answered, misunderstanding her.

"No. I mean, it's okay." She sighed. "I mean, you're not in our way." She closed her eyes and took another deep breath. She looked him in the eye, and her request came rushing out. "I was wondering if you could help us pick out a toy for my friend's puppy? She just got him for her birthday, and I wanted to get a toy for him, but I don't know anything about what toys puppies might like. I mean, do we get a squeaky toy? A fuzzy toy? A bone? Ack! Too many choices!" She was talking fast, and Leah knew she was worried he might think she was weird.

The man's face relaxed into a grin, and he nodded. "I understand the dilemma. There *are* a lot of choices." He looked at the wall of toys before looking back at Lucy and Micah. "Do you know what kind of puppy she has?"

Lucy's face fell. "Does that matter?"

"Not necessarily. All puppies need good chew toys. Something like this—" He grabbed a soft monkey that was holding pieces of rope between his hands and feet. "—would be great. The puppy can chew on the rope, but it's also something your friend can use to interact with her puppy, too, which helps them bond."

"That sounds perfect, sir, thank you!" Leah accepted the toy and put it in their own cart. "Would you like a candy cane?" She held the candy out to him.

He took the candy cane and put it in his pocket. "Thank you," he said, his voice thick. "I haven't had one of these in a very long time." He glanced at the three of them. "You all have a Merry Christmas." He turned back to his cart and pushed it down the aisle.

Lucy and Micah high-fived as Leah beamed at them. She grabbed the toy from the cart to hang it back up.

"Wait, Mama. Can we get that for me to give to Alaina?"

"Oh, right. You *do* happen to have a friend with a new puppy." Leah examined the toy in her hand. "Okay."

December 4

Dear Lucy and Micah,

I could see you enjoyed finding opportunities to ask for help so you could give out a candy cane. That was so fun to watch! Before school today, I want you to go through the stickers I bought and pick out one for each classmate. You can also choose some for other people you see at school.

Love,

Mama

"OHH, RUEBEN WOULD LOVE THIS one!" exclaimed Micah, grabbing a sticker of a dog playing baseball. "And Olivia would like this one!"

"Oh! Alaina, Jules, and Mari would love these." Lucy picked up some sparkly stickers. She picked up a few more, mumbling names as she went.

"I'm glad you like the choices," laughed Leah.

"These are great." Lucy stopped for a moment. "Do I *have* to give the boys stickers, too?"

"Hey! I'm a boy, and I like stickers!" Micah was indignant.

"It's not that, bubby," explained Lucy. "It's just, *ugh*, the boys at school are dumb. Well, not *dumb*, but not usually very nice to some of us."

Leah rested her hand on Lucy's shoulder. "Yes. You can be kind, even if they are . . ." She thought for a moment. "What are they doing now?"

"They try to keep from touching one of the girls, saying she has a disease. They talk during class when we're trying to listen to the teacher. They ask to borrow a pencil but then break it before giving it back."

"Yeah, not nice is right. You can still practice kindness, even within boundaries you set."

"Like what?"

"Well, instead of letting them borrow a pencil, you can give them one and tell them to keep it—*before* they break it. But you don't have to give them pencils if you don't have any to spare or even if you just don't feel like it that day. Sometimes people behave like that because they have feelings or emotions that they don't understand or know how to handle. Sometimes it's something totally unrelated to the people around them receiving the meanness. That doesn't excuse it, though. Being kind doesn't mean being a doormat. If it gets to be something that makes you uncomfortable or unsafe, rather than just annoyed or irritated, talk to your teacher or me or your principal. Okay?"

"Yeah, they're not mean like that. More obnoxious

than anything. Mrs. W told them they're not allowed to ask us for pencils anymore, though." Lucy smirked. "Jules told them whatever disease they think Sophie has couldn't be half as bad as what they have."

"What do they have?" asked Micah, looking up from the stickers spread across the table.

"Don't take this the wrong way, bubby. Jules told them they have 'stupid boy syndrome.'"

"Hey!" Micah crossed his arms and glared at Lucy.

"Not you, Micah! Not all boys have it. Just those boys! The boys who aren't nice." She slid her arm around her little brother and squeezed. "You're nice. You don't have it."

"Lucy-girl, all kids go through a phase of figuring things out. They struggle with knowing how to be kind or when to have extra kindness. Once you've figured it out, it might seem 'stupid' that someone else hasn't figured it out yet, but they'll get it—*hopefully*. In the meantime, you don't have to respond to or engage with the stuff that isn't okay." Leah considered her daughter's heart. "Or if there's something else you'd rather do . . ." she trailed off.

Lucy shook her head. "I think you're right, Mama. I need to just ignore them when they're like that. Except maybe when they're saying something that's actually mean, like about Sophie having a disease." She rolled her eyes and shook her head. "It's so dumb." She placed her hand on Micah's shoulder. When his eyes met hers, she gave strict orders. "Don't ever be like that, Micah. Seriously. Never."

December 5

Dear Lucy and Micah,

I bet your friends were excited to get the stickers you picked out for each of them. Did their eyes light up? Today, let's make some of Daddy's favorite cookies to deliver with the pictures you made.

Love,

Mama

"REMEMBER HOW DADDY TRIES—TRIED—to eat all the frosting before we could put it on the cookies?" Lucy giggled.

"And Mommy always told him no cookie dough." Micah laughed as he remembered. "That's why he'd eat the frosting."

"That—and it's *yummy*!" Lucy leaned into Leah. "So. Yummy."

Leah grinned as she wiped the flour from her daughter's nose and swiped it across Micah's cheek. "You have a little something on your cheek, bubs."

Micah stuck his finger in the bowl beside him and rubbed it against Leah's cheek. "You do, too, Mama."

Leah used her finger to get the frosting off her face and tasted it. "Perfect." She rubbed noses with Micah. "Thanks for the sample."

"Can I have a taste?" Micah's eyes brightened at the thought of sampling the frosting.

"Grab a spoon. We shouldn't keep putting our fingers in it." Lucy opened her mouth, but Leah stopped her. "You, too." Leah grinned.

As each pulled out a spoonful of frosting, Lucy leaned against the counter. "Mama? Most of my friends talk about cutting out sugar cookies at Christmas. Could we try that?" She took a lick of frosting from her spoon.

"We could probably try that a different day. This dough is very soft, even if we put it in the fridge, so we make balls and flatten them instead."

"Oh." Disappointment flitted across Lucy's face. "What kind of dough do we need?"

"Well, one with not as much flour. This one makes super soft and fluffy cookies that kind of melt in your mouth. The kind of cookies you're thinking of aren't quite as soft. Still yummy, though." Leah pulled out her recipe binder and flipped to a page. "Here's the one we'd need if we made cut-outs."

Micah peered at the page. "'Aunt Dot's Cut-Out Sugar Cookies'?" he read. "Who's Aunt Dot again?"

"She's your grandpa's sister. She gave me this recipe several years ago. Sometimes I make her cookies instead of these." Leah handed them the recipe they were using.

"'Sue's Melt in Your Mouth Sugar Cookies.' Who's Sue?" asked Lucy. "I've never heard of her."

"Sue is a wonderful lady I knew before I met your daddy. We went to church together, and her cookies were *always* a hit." Leah bent down and dropped her voice to a whisper. "Sometimes they were given as prizes for contests—that's how great they are." She stood back up, her eyes filling with tears. "When your daddy and I had to move for his job, she gave me her recipe. Daddy liked the soft cookies better than cut-outs, but I'm not sure why. That's why I've made these every year."

"Well," said Lucy as she snagged a cooled cookie from the rack, "these *are* pretty yummy."

December 6

Dear Lucy and Micah,

The Davidsons from church had their baby a few days ago! Emilee and Isaac have a new little brother. I would like you to help me make a meal for them and deliver it this evening.

Love,

Mama

"LEAH!" DUSTIN'S WEARY FACE BRIGHTENED as he answered the door.

"Good evening, Dustin." Leah smiled as she turned to Lucy and Micah. "The kids wanted to bring you a meal this evening. They helped slice the veggies and picked up the sauce."

"It's tza-tza-tzatziki sauce." Lucy beamed with pride in saying it. "We made sheet pan chicken!"

Dustin leaned against the doorframe as he looked through the pan's lid. "Oooh. Chicken, onions, and peppers? Delicious." Two little faces peeked around him. "Emilee, Isaac? Can you tell them thank you?"

The two-year-old pulled her thumb from her mouth and wrapped her arms around Dustin's leg. "Fanks."

Micah held out a plate to the five-year-old dark-haired boy still standing behind Dustin. Leah rubbed her hand down the back of Micah's head. She squatted down to eye-level with Isaac.

"Do you like brownies?"

His head bobbed.

"Then I guess it's good we made some." She smiled and handed him the plate. "Do you want to take this inside for Daddy?"

He accepted the plate and turned to run to the kitchen. "Thank you!" he called as ran off, Emilee trailing behind him.

"Thank you so much for dinner, Leah. I had to go back to work today, and I hate not being able to be home to do more. Josie's a trooper, and thankfully baby Graham is eating and sleeping well. My mom is keeping Emilee and Isaac for a few weeks so Josie can rest. We weren't expecting a c-section, though, so Josie thought she'd be up and moving sooner after delivery like she was with Emilee."

"I'd love to help out, Dustin. Will you or Josie text me after the kids are in bed and let me know what days would be best for me to come over? My schedule—"

"The house is a mess, Leah," interrupted Dustin. "We can't really have company."

Leah blinked and put her hand to her chest. "Oh, not as company. Heavens, no!" She shook her head. "No, I want to come over and help with the house. Josie needs to rest. I know how to do laundry and clean toilets. I've even used a vacuum once or twice."

"I don't know if . . ." He trailed off.

"Please," Leah paused. "Let me do this. No judgment. None. I've been there, and I understand."

Dustin nodded. "Okay." His eyes shone with tears as he bit his lip to keep them from falling. "Thank you."

"I'm glad I could help out tonight. I'm more than happy to have Isaac and Emilee over to play for a few hours, too."

Lucy tapped Leah's shoulder.

"Yes?"

Lucy pointed to herself and mouthed something.

"I'm not sure what you're saying."

Lucy whispered in Leah's ear. "Oh! Yes!"

Dustin watched the exchange with a bemused expression. "Everything okay?"

"Yes, yes, it is." Leah beamed with pride at her daughter. "I'd nearly forgotten that Lucy has been through babysitter training and is CPR and first aid certified."

Lucy nodded and grinned.

"Oh, that's nice, but I don't know if we need—" Dustin broke off mid-thought.

Lucy blinked. "Mr. Davidson? I start school break at the end of next week, and I'd love to be able to come help out with Emilee and Isaac a few days during break. I can even make lunch! And you don't have to pay me. I just want to help."

"Oh. Well, that would be very nice, Lucy, thank you." Dustin reached up and scratched the back of his head. "Everyone has been so helpful."

"People helped us when we needed it earlier this year. And sometimes even now. Like letting us help you. That helps us, too." Leah grinned. "Oh! And if it's okay, I'd love to take Emilee and Isaac with us to see the lights at the zoo when we go. That'll give you and Josie some time together to just focus on each other and baby Graham."

"That's so generous, Leah, thank you."

"It's my pleasure, Dustin. We'll talk to you soon." She put her hands on Lucy and Micah's shoulders and steered them toward their car. "Have a good night, Dustin," she called over her shoulder.

December 7

Dear Lucy and Micah,

Today's the day! It's time to deliver the pictures and cookies to neighbors. I want to make sure we take some to Mr. Johnson next door. Who else do you think we can deliver to?

Love,
Mama

LUCY AND LEAH COVERED THE plates of cookies with cling wrap, and Micah topped each plate with a bow. They had lined up the plates on the counter. Leah silently thanked God for no snow so they could use their wagon to haul the cookies.

"Besides Mr. Johnson, who else should we take cookies to?" asked Leah.

Lucy stacked the pictures together and slid each one into a folder with a bow. "Miss Carol?"

"Great idea," agreed Leah.

"What about Mr. and Mrs. Hamilton, Mommy?" Micah wondered aloud. "I bet they would like some!"

"I think you're probably right, Micah." Leah ruffled Micah's hair. It had gotten darker this year—not as blonde as hers, but closer to Jacob's color. He looked more like Jacob every day: a sweet reminder of the man she loved. "I think we should visit the Knutsons and the Mongs, as well."

"Oh!" exclaimed Lucy. "We need to take some to the Sheppards, too."

"Sounds like a plan to me."

The trio put on their coats and made their way outside, each precariously balancing cookies. Leah had the added task of carrying the pictures, which she'd tucked under her arm. "Micah? Will you set the cookies here and get the wagon from the garage?"

Micah plopped the cookies on the patio table and went in the side door to the garage. A moment later, he pulled the wagon behind him. "Here we go!" He took the folders from Leah and spread them out in the wagon. He placed his plates in the wagon, then helped Leah arrange all the plates so they fit and wouldn't slide around.

Lucy hummed and danced as they started their walk, bursting into song as they walked up Mr. Johnson's sidewalk. "We wish you a Merry Christmas, and a Happy New Year!"

Micah giggled at his sister's dancing as he pulled the wagon, careful not to hit any rocks on the sidewalk.

"Can I knock, Mama?"

Leah nodded and handed Lucy a plate of cookies and a picture folder, watching as Lucy rapped her knuckles on the blue door in front of them and stepped back as it started to open.

"Oh, hello there, Bowers family."

"Hi, Mr. Johnson. We brought you some cookies." Lucy held out the plate.

"That's thoughtful of you, thank you." He peeked at the cookies. "Are those your mama's famous sugar cookies?"

"Yep!" piped up Micah. "Daddy's favorite!"

"Well, that is pretty great."

"They taste *awesome*, too." Micah tugged on Leah's arm. When she leaned down, he whispered, "Can I go to Miss Carol's now?"

Leah nodded and whispered back, "Yes, have Lucy go with you."

Micah grabbed Lucy's hand and pulled. "Lucy! Come with me to Miss Carol's house. Pleeeease."

Lucy followed him, and Leah turned to Mr. Johnson. "How are you?"

"It's weird not having dad around this year, but I'm doing okay." He cocked his head to the side. "What about you?"

Leah knew the smile she gave him didn't quite meet her eyes. "I'm managing. Some days are harder than others." She sighed and eyed her children talking to Miss Carol next door, Lucy's hands animated in the conversation. "Trying to bring him into the things we're doing for others this month, hoping it helps them remember him."

Mr. Johnson nodded. "What a good idea for keeping his memory alive during the holidays." He watched the kids, who were laughing with Miss Carol. "It seems like they're doing okay today."

"Today's a good day. They've had some giggles."

"You're doing a good job, Leah. You probably don't hear that enough now."

She swallowed a sob. "Thank you." She offered him a hug. "We'll see you later. We have a couple more houses to get to."

December 8

Dear Lucy and Micah,

Today, I would like each of you to write a letter to mail to your grandma and great-grandma. You can tell them whatever you want, but no asking for presents or anything else.

Love,

Mama

LEAH STARED OUT THE KITCHEN window as the kids worked on their letters. Predictably, Micah had finished quickly and ran off to play. Lucy's pencil scratched against the paper as she wrote, bringing a smile to Leah's face.

Lucy appeared next to her. "Mama?"

Leah turned, surprised yet again at how grown up her twelve-year-old seemed. "Yes, my sweet girl?"

Lucy grinned and hugged Leah before continuing.

"Is it okay if I tell Mimi about Micah's karate tournament coming up? She might want to come visit then."

"Hmmm." Leah thought for a moment. "Yes, but . . ." Leah held up a finger. "Don't ask her to come. This letter is just supposed to let her know you're thinking about her."

"Okay." Lucy started back to the table. "I love writing letters. Maybe I'll write more."

"That would be great. I know she'd love to hear from you more."

"I meant maybe I'd write a few for other people." Lucy looked up from her letter. "Is that okay?"

Leah's face brightened. "Absolutely! But not this afternoon." She placed her hand on the table beside the letter.

Lucy frowned. "Why not?"

"We're taking Isaac and Emilee Davidson to the zoo."

"Oh, yeah! I forgot about that."

"It's okay." Leah reached for the envelope Lucy had already addressed to her great-grandma. "We'll drop these in the mail on our way there. We're staying to see the lights tonight."

Lucy looked down at her letter, thinking. "Mama? Why are we doing that?" she asked, looking up to search Leah's face.

Leah tilted her head to study her daughter. "What do you mean? Doing what?"

"I guess, well, I mean. Yeesh. I guess I don't understand."

"What don't you understand, sweetheart?"

Lucy chewed the top of her pen before answering. "I know we took them food because they had a new baby, and it was a nice thing to do. But I heard you tell Mr. Davidson that you'd come help clean around the house, and today, we're taking Emilee and Isaac to the zoo with us? It's not like they're our cousins or something. I mean, I don't mind them coming. I just don't get why you're doing it." Lucy's head dropped. "I guess that sounds really selfish."

Leah sat next to Lucy and lifted her chin. "Lucy, it doesn't sound selfish. It just sounds like you don't understand."

"I don't." She crossed her arms and leaned back in her chair.

"Lucy, God has called us to love one another, right?" When Lucy nodded, Leah continued. "He even tells us that no greater love does one have than to lay down your life for your friends."

Lucy drew in a breath and sat up, her bottom lip pulled between her teeth.

"But very seldom are we confronted with the choice of literally dying for our friend."

Lucy let out her breath and slumped in her seat as Leah went on.

"However, giving up something we want in order to help our friend is a sacrifice, which is what He really wants from us. For example, I don't really like cleaning—our house or anyone else's." Leah scrunched up her face.

Lucy laughed but promptly sobered. "Then why did you tell them you'd help?"

"Because, dear daughter, I remember how hard it can be with a new baby in the house. And baby Graham has *two* older siblings, which makes it extra hard. If I can do something—even if it's something I don't enjoy—to help, why wouldn't I do that?"

Lucy looked like a Cheshire cat, her grin wide across her face. "Is it like dying because you're *dying* inside when you're cleaning?"

Leah moaned. "Probably." She laughed. "You did the same thing, though."

Lucy lifted her left eyebrow. "I didn't offer to clean their house, Mama."

Leah chuckled. "No, but you offered to give up some of your Christmas break to help out at their house. I know you were planning on a relaxing Christmas break. Instead, you'll be playing with two little ones." Leah reached for her daughter and embraced her. "I'm so, so proud of you."

"Yeah, yeah, whatever," Lucy mumbled as she returned the hug.

December 9

Dear Lucy and Micah,

    Today, we're going to try something new. I would like for us to get Christmas cards for everyone at the rescue mission. Lucy can call to find out how many we need, and Micah can help pick out cards.

    Love,

    Mama

THE TRIO STOOD IN FRONT of the display, trying to decide which cards to purchase. "I guess it would help if you call and ask them how many we need, wouldn't it?" asked Leah, handing her phone to Lucy.

Lucy took a deep breath and dialed the number. "Hi, my name's Lucy and me and my brother want to bring Christmas cards for everyone who comes there. Could you please tell me how many we need?" Lucy listened to the other end. Her eyes widened. "Did you say two *hundred*?"

Micah and Leah looked at each other, their eyes big.

"Okay, thank you." Lucy waited, listening. "I'm not sure when we'll bring them, but yes, we'll call before we do." She ended the call and handed Leah the phone. "They said two hundred."

"I heard." Leah laughed. "A few more than what I was expecting, but that's okay. We can do this."

Lucy's brow furrowed, and a look of confusion crossed her face. "Mama?"

"Yes?"

"She said they don't usually get individual cards for people who are there, and that it's very kind that we want to do this. She said businesses usually send one card for them to hang for everyone to see." Lucy drew a deep breath. "Why don't they send one for each person? Don't they think people would want their own?"

"I'm not sure, Lucy-girl. If I had to guess, I'd say they probably just don't think about it."

Micah piped up. "Could you imagine signing two *hundred* cards?" His face fell. "Oh, wait."

Leah mussed his hair. "Maybe we can have some friends help us sign some cards."

"Mama!" Micah patted his head. "Let's do this! We need . . ." He looked at one of the boxes of cards and started counting on his fingers. "Um, I forgot. I don't know my times tables that high."

Leah laughed with him. "Let's look. How many does each box have?"

"This one has twelve," said Micah, handing Leah a box.

"This one has ten," added Lucy, holding a box up with her left hand. She waved her right hand. "But this one has twenty."

"Ohh," said Leah. "I like that. Let's look for boxes of twenty."

"But how many boxes?" asked Micah.

Leah knelt to be eye-to-eye with her son. "How many times do you think twenty goes into two hundred?"

"I don't know!" yelled Micah, frustrated.

Leah set the box of cards back on the shelf and held Micah's hands, rubbing the backs of them. "It's okay if you don't know." She took a deep breath. "We'll figure it out together." She let out the breath slowly. "Let's think about it for a minute." She took another deep breath and held it. Micah mimicked her this time. She held up four fingers, putting them down one at a time slowly. They both released their breaths.

Micah closed his eyes and took another deep breath. Leah waited while Lucy continued to look for twenty-count boxes of cards. A few seconds later, Micah blew out slowly. "Ten. We need ten boxes." His eyes flew open. "Is that right?"

Leah nodded as tears flooded her eyes. She knew he

struggled with regulating his emotions, but this time, Micah had calmed himself down.

"Good job, bubby!" cried Lucy.

Micah laughed. "I just realized it was a tens problem, 'cause it had a zero at the end. I'm so weird."

They counted out ten boxes before picking out an extra box "just in case" and heading to the front of the store to pay.

Micah nearly skipped to the cashier. "We need two hundred cards, so we got ten boxes of twenty." He lowered his voice and nodded. "I did the math."

"Good job, little man." The teenage cashier looked suitably impressed and offered a fist bump, which Micah promptly gave him.

December 10

Dear Lucy and Micah,

One of Daddy's favorite things for us to do was ride around and look at lights. Today, we'll decorate our outside trees and the windows for other people to see our lights.

Love,

Mama

"HOW'S THIS LOOK, MAMA?" LUCY held a wreath up to the kitchen window.

"I like it!" Leah helped her hang it before walking outside with Micah. The crisp air felt cool against her face, and she blinked at the bright sky. She shivered as she zipped her coat.

"Mama?"

"Hmm?"

"Can we put lights on the fence, too?"

Micah's face held hope, and Leah couldn't resist.

"We can try. I think some of the clips we bought will work for that." She mussed his hair. "We'll find out together."

"Mama?"

"Yes, bubs?"

"What do you get when you cross a snowman with a vampire?"

"Umm . . . I don't know."

"Frostbite." Micah burst into giggles.

Leah laughed with him and gave him a hug.

"I have one, too, Mama." Lucy tugged the hood of her pink winter coat over her head. "What do snowmen eat for lunch?"

"I *know* that one already," whined Micah as he pulled on his mittens. "Frosted Flakes."

"Nope," smirked Lucy. "That's what they eat for breakfast."

"Hmm." Leah thought out loud: "What do snowmen eat for lunch? Umm, cold cuts?"

"That would work, but nope. They eat . . . pause for dramatic effect." Lucy took a breath while Micah and Leah waited. "Iceberg-ers." Lucy gave an exaggerated nod as the other two groaned.

"Oh, brother," said Micah. "I mean, oh, sister."

"My turn." Leah's eyes sparkled as she waited for them to stop giggling. "Okay, knock knock."

"Who's there?" they chorused together.

"Yah."

Micah and Lucy looked at each other, puzzled. "Yah who?"

"Wow! You two are really excited for Christmas!"

Micah threw his head back. "Yaaaaahooooooo!" he shouted, grinning.

Leah watched Lucy and Micah run outside, chasing each other around the yard. She loved hearing their laughter and watching them play. They seemed to have a lightness about them—a lightness that she was still trying to find in her grief. Grief was like that, though: waves of joy and waves of sadness. Missing Jacob like she was missing an arm but still going through her day. She caught up with Micah. "Are you ready to light up our fence?"

December 11

Dear Lucy and Micah,

The house looks beautiful. Having lights twinkling on our fence was a great idea, Micah. Lucy, I love how you decorated each of the trees in our yard with a different color of lights. You've worked so hard to get it ready for Christmas this year. Today, we're going to help out at our church and the neighborhood around it by picking up trash. I have bags and gloves for us to use. We want to get the trash picked up before the snow comes and buries it!

Love,
Mama

LEAH HANDED LUCY AND MICAH each a bag and waved them to the bathroom to change. "You're not wearing church clothes to pick up trash."

"Thanks, Mama. I don't want to get my dress icky from the dirt and trash."

"You're welcome, sweetheart. Hurry and change. Everyone's heading out, and they want to lock up."

Lucy rushed to the bathroom and changed, reappearing a few minutes later. Micah was by the front door and ready to go.

"Thanks for being so fast!" Leah held open the front door of the church as they left the building. They dropped their church clothes in the car and retrieved their bags and gloves. "I also have wipes, so when we're all done, we'll clean up a little and go get some lunch."

"Yes!" shouted Micah. "Can we get Wendy's?"

"We'll see," answered Leah. She looked around. "Let's walk around the church first and see what might need to be picked up. Some outside groups use the building, too, so we want to make sure that it looks welcoming for everyone, not just for Sunday mornings."

A few minutes later, they'd collected a few items around the church and started walking down the street. They came to the stop sign, where there was a pile of discarded fast-food bags, empty soda cans, and napkins.

"Yuck!" Lucy scrunched her nose and shuddered. "Why is there so much trash here?" She glanced down the street. "And along the sidewalk?"

"I think sometimes people aren't thinking about the mess it leaves behind when they throw things out their car window or drop it when they're walking. I *also* think that people don't always realize when something blows out of their car or falls out of their pocket," answered Leah.

"Maybe we'll find some dog poop," laughed Micah. "That would be awesome. Poop. Right, Lucy?"

"Gross! No, Micah! That would not be awesome!"

"Do NOT pick up dog poop, Micah Liam Bowers! Absolutely not."

"But—"

"No buts. No poop."

Micah giggled as he mimicked Leah under his breath. "No butts, no poop." He said it louder. "No butts, no poop. Get it, Lucy? No *butts*, no *poop*?"

Lucy started to chuckle before stopping herself. "Yes, Micah. I get it. I just don't think it's funny." She pursed her lips to keep from laughing.

Leah rolled her eyes. "Oh geez." She shook her head, laughing. "Funny, Micah, funny."

He pointed to her. "*You* said it, Mommy! Daddy would be crying from laughing so much right now."

Lucy snickered. "Yeah, he would. He'd never let you live it down, either."

"Yeah, yeah." Leah trailed off, smiling to herself at how much they had enjoyed Jacob's sense of humor. Which included all the poop jokes Micah loved.

December 12

Dear Lucy and Micah,

I can't believe we picked up a whole bag of trash in a one-block area! Great job, you two! Today, we are making explosion boxes for your teachers' Christmas presents. We'll put some candy and gift cards in there for you to give them for Christmas.

Love,

Mama

"AM I MAKING ONE FOR *all* of my teachers, Mama?" Lucy's eyes were wide and her forehead wrinkled. The small family sat at their dining table with cardstock spread all over. "I have so many this year. That'll take me all day!"

"I have boxes already made, so we can use some of them. How about you make one for your *favorite*, and we'll use my boxes for the others?"

Relief flooded her face. "Okay." She looked at the colors and designs of paper in front of her. "What if I don't know her favorite color?"

"Well, you can always do a Christmas one." Leah felt a tap on her shoulder and turned, smiling. "Yes, Micah?"

"Miss Paula's favorite color is turquoise."

Leah hugged her son. "How'd you know that?"

"Uh . . . her purse is turquoise, she has a turquoise lantern in our classroom, she has a turquoise bag she carries books in, and her coat is turquoise." Micah smirked as he pointed out the obvious. "Oh. And her dog's name is Turk. Like 'turk-woise.'"

"Good observation skills, Micah." Leah grinned. "Which pieces would you like to use for her box? All turquoise? Or do you want to do Christmassy green and red? Or turquoise and something else?"

"Hmmm." Micah tapped his finger on his cheek as he thought.

Leah held her breath, remembering all the times she'd seen Jacob do that very thing.

"Maybe Christmas colors on the inside? But mostly turquoise, especially for the outside box."

"Sounds good, bubba." Sadness tinged her words. She'd cry later. She swallowed a sob. "What should we put on the inside? We can do fun-sized candy bars, gift cards, or any other small-ish things you might want to put in there."

"Mama? Can I make a bracelet to put in mine?"

Leah smiled at Lucy's thoughtfulness. "You sure can."

"Mommy, can I put some candy bars in mine?" asked Micah. "Oh! Be right back!" He ran from the room and came back with his fist closed. "I have some dollar coins I want to add."

"That's sweet of you, Micah. Your teachers will like that." Leah held out her hand as he released the money into it. "What gift cards should we get?"

"Starbucks, for sure," said Lucy. "All of my teachers love their coffee from Starbucks."

"Miss Paula likes Aut-to Mocha."

"Okay, coffee gift cards for everyone." Leah wrote it down to remember to buy later. "What do you guys think about the little tags from Wendy's to get a free Frosty?"

"I *love* Frostys. I say yes."

Lucy nodded her head in agreement. "Good idea, Mama. What about cards to Sweet Tooth?"

"Oh, yeah." Leah's mouth watered as she thought about the homemade sweet shop. She added it to her list with the key tags from Wendy's and tapped her pen as she thought. "Lucy?"

Lucy looked up from gluing the smallest box together. "Yeah?"

"What do you think of doing an animated Post-it pad?"

Lucy chewed her bottom lip as she considered the

idea. "That's a lot. Six teachers. I don't know if I'll have time."

"How about just for your favorite?" Leah winked at Lucy and leaned toward her. "I was thinking you could do something in the corner or along the bottom edge, like someone pushing a broom across the bottom or a dog that sits in the corner."

Lucy's eyes brightened. "I can do someone walking back and forth across the bottom. They could even look up." She grinned. "That's the first one Daddy taught me how to draw, and I'll be able to get it done before I give it to her." She jumped up and put her arms around Leah. "Thanks, Mama."

December 13

LEAH SAT ON THE COUCH, tendrils of hair hanging around her face. "That was fun!" exclaimed Lucy as she bounced onto the seat beside Leah.

"And hot!" added Micah.

"I can't believe it had to be almost *three hundred degrees* before it was done." Lucy leaned against Leah. "No wonder you didn't want us to do the stirring or pouring part."

Leah slid her arm around Lucy. "It does get a bit warm. I have some special gloves I use when I'm making a lot."

"Mama?" Micah slid onto Leah's lap, and she put her arms around his waist. When she raised her eyebrows, he continued. "Who is the brittle for?"

She squeezed him and kissed his cheek. "I haven't really decided yet. Who do you think it should go to?"

He scrunched up his face, then broke into a grin. "Do we have to give it to anyone? I mean, *I* like brittle, especially since there's bacon in it. *Yum.*"

"Micah!" Lucy growled. "We can't keep it! We made it for other people!"

Leah patted Lucy's knee. "It's okay, Lucy. We made enough that we can keep some for ourselves." She gave Micah a pointed look. "But we have plenty to give to others, too."

Lucy stood and stretched. "Mama? Why did Daddy like this brittle so much?"

"Well," began Leah, "that's how we met, for one. I was delivering brittle to a friend, and your daddy happened to be there. We all talked for a little bit before I had to go. After I left, he asked JJ, my friend, if we were dating. JJ teased him and told him that he was getting ready to ask me to marry him but stopped when he realized your daddy really wanted to ask me out. He offered your daddy a piece of the brittle. Your daddy had never tried maple bacon pecan brittle before." She smiled at the memory. "JJ told Daddy that he'd ask me about giving out my number. Daddy told him to make sure he asked for more of the brittle, too."

"Wait a second!" interjected Micah. "Are you talking about Uncle JJ?"

Leah nodded as she chuckled. "Yep. He said that since he got to play matchmaker, he should be Uncle JJ and have a free lifetime supply of brittle."

"He's so funny." Micah stood up. "Oh! Maybe we should give it to him!"

"Great idea. We'll figure out who else would enjoy it."

"Mama?"

"Yes, Lucy?"

"Where did Daddy take you for your first date?"

Leah twirled a strand of hair as she remembered. "We went to this soup place that isn't there anymore." She closed her eyes and drew a breath. "I can almost smell it." She opened her eyes. "It was this awesome place that had so many soups, some bread, and just a few sandwiches. There were so many choices! We were there for probably three hours, then we went to Millie's Diner for dessert."

"He didn't take you to the movies?!"

The incredulity in Lucy's voice made Leah giggle. "No. We thought about it, but we were having such a good time talking that we decided to skip the movie. We laughed so much just in our conversation. I don't think I would've had that at a movie."

"Daddy is—was—pretty funny."

"Yeah, he was."

December 14

Dear Lucy and Micah,

I'm glad you enjoyed making brittle with me yesterday. Today, you're going to hang out with Aunt Shelly while I go to the Davidsons' to help Miss Josie. While you're with Aunt Shelly, please see what you can do to help her at her house.

Love,

Mama

"WE GET TO GO TO Aunt Shelly's! We get to go to Aunt Shelly's!" Lucy and Micah held hands and jumped around in a circle in the kitchen as Leah stood at the stove.

"Excited, are we?" Leah couldn't hold back her smile. She loved seeing her children excited to spend time with her sister.

"Only like . . ." Lucy held her fingers about a half inch apart. "This much!" She threw her arms far apart.

"I'd never have guessed," murmured Leah under her breath.

"What was that, Mama?" asked Lucy.

"Nothing." Leah finished breakfast and set their plates on the table. "Let's eat so we can get movin'."

"God, thank You for this food. Amen!" Micah was quick and to the point. Leah raised an eyebrow as he started eating. "What? I'm hungry!"

Leah's shoulders shook with laughter as she sat with them. "Do you have any ideas about what you might do for Aunt Shelly?"

"You know the peanut butter cookie recipe I love?" asked Lucy. Leah nodded, and Lucy continued. "I thought I might make some of those for her while we're there, if you'll let me take the monkfruit."

"That's a great idea! I love that you remember Aunt Shelly is diabetic, so we want to be careful of the sugar. She loves those cookies, too. Remember to keep them in just a little longer than usual."

"Mm-hmm." Lucy mumbled as she ate a bite of pancake.

"I want to run the sweeper!"

"Of course you do, Micah." Leah grinned. Vacuuming and Swiffering were Micah's two favorite chores. "Do you want to take your headphones with you, so it won't be too loud?"

"Oh, yeah!"

Micah stood to get them, but Leah stopped him.

"Breakfast first, bubba."

"Right," he said as he plopped into his seat. He used his fork to cut off a piece of sausage and dipped it in syrup before putting it in his mouth. "Hmpf-ef-ifhishush."

"Do you wanna try that again without food in your mouth?" asked Leah, amused.

Micah made a show of chewing his sausage and swallowing it. He took a drink and gave Leah two thumbs up. "This is delicious."

"Sausage and syrup?"

"Yep! Exactly how Daddy told me I should eat it. The syrup is perfect for making the sausage sweeter."

Overcome with giggles, Leah nodded. "Yeah, syrup would do that."

"Do you like syrup with *your* sausages, Mommy?" asked Micah.

Leah scrunched up her face. "It's not really my cup of tea."

"That's cause it's syrup, not tea."

"I just mean no, I don't really like it." Leah frowned when Micah's face fell. "It's okay for you to like it and for me not to. I won't yuck your yum."

Lucy shrugged. "It's okay. Not my favorite."

Micah stared at her. "Of course it's not. You put ketchup on *everything*." He gave her a look that dared her to disagree.

"True story, bro."

The siblings dissolved into giggles.

December 15

Dear Lucy and Micah,

Aunt Shelly is grateful for the help you gave her with the floors, Micah. And Lucy, she texted me late last night that she was making a midnight snack out of your cookies. She enjoyed her time with you yesterday, especially playing Taco Cat Goat Cheese Pizza. Today, you're spending time with Aunt Teresa, Aunt Darla, and Uncle Jon. Sometimes the greatest gift we can give is listening. I hope that, today, you will ask your aunts and uncle about what Daddy was like growing up. And then <u>listen</u>.

Love,

Mama

LUCY AND MICAH WERE LAUGHING as they climbed into the car. "It sounds like you had a good time today."

"Did you know that Daddy used to beg Grandma to make sugar cookies every year at this time?" asked Lucy, her blonde ponytail bouncing.

"Yeah," continued Micah, "but Aunt Teresa said Grandma wasn't a very good baker, so every year, they were either burnt or yucky to eat."

Leah found herself giggling with her children. "I didn't know that, but I bet that's why he always wanted to eat the frosting and not wait for cookies."

Lucy's jaw dropped. "I bet you're right, Mama. That makes a lot of sense."

"Daddy also used to cheat anytime he played games with Uncle Jon," snickered Micah.

"Like someone else I know," mumbled Lucy.

"I do not cheat!" hollered Micah.

"How do you know I was talking about you then?"

Micah slumped against his seat and folded his arms across his chest. "Whatever."

"Okay, you two." Leah shook her head. "He told me about that. Uncle Jon almost always set up games in his favor, drawing from the bottom of card piles or dealing himself the best cards."

"Like Lucy," whispered Micah.

"Micah." Leah's voice held a warning.

"Uncle Jon told us that part, too." Lucy frowned. "He said at first he did it to be funny cause Daddy would get mad, but he stopped when he realized Daddy was *really* angry. But Daddy didn't stop when Uncle Jon did. Uncle Jon let him do it anyway."

"Aunt Darla said she used to dress Daddy up like her doll," giggled Micah from the backseat, his hands covering his mouth.

"She said he wasn't a very pretty girl," added Lucy. "Aunt Teresa agreed with her."

Leah smirked. "I can imagine he wasn't."

"Aunt Teresa said she took her role of oldest *very* seriously. Did you know she taught Daddy a lot about drawing?"

"Yes, I did," confessed Leah. "He always said Aunt Teresa taught him more than he learned at school, just because she started teaching him when he was wee little."

"That's pretty cool." Lucy quieted and pulled something out of her coat. "I asked her to draw something for me." She passed the paper to Leah. "She drew me riding a unicorn. It's *really* good." She pursed her lips. "I wonder why she isn't a designer like Daddy?"

"Aunt Teresa still creates a lot of art. I think she even teaches some private classes for kids every now and then. She loved numbers, too, though, so she became an accountant. She's brilliant at both."

"Mama? Would it be okay if Aunt Teresa helps me with my art? Could we ask her?"

"I think that's a fantastic idea, Lucy-girl. I'll call her when we get home. I bet she'd love to."

December 16

Dear Lucy and Micah,

You gave a great gift to Aunt Teresa, Aunt Darla, and Uncle Jon simply by listening. I know they miss their brother, so I'm sure talking about him made them happy.

Today, I want you to plan a birthday party for Jesus. We celebrate His birthday this time of year, so you should plan something fun to invite your friends to. Think of what you can do that would be a good way to celebrate.

Love,

Mama

LEAH SAT AT HER COUNTER, sipping coffee while she read through her morning devotions. A door opened in the hall and the sound of paper being torn split the air. Another door opened, feet padding into a bedroom.

Leah tiptoed in close to listen as Micah woke Lucy to read the note.

"Yes!" Micah hissed as Lucy finished reading their note. "I love parties. We have to have cupcakes!"

"Shhh!" Lucy shushed him. "Mama's still asleep!"

Leah smiled, appreciating Lucy's thoughtfulness.

"Oh, yeah," whispered Micah. Leah heard him climbed onto Lucy's bed. "We have to have cupcakes!"

"Maybe we should wait for Mama," worried Lucy.

"You said it says she wants *us* to plan it. We should start now." Micah was matter-of-fact.

"I don't know, Micah—"

"Please, Lucy?" Leah imagined him folding his hands under his chin and looking up at her, eyes wide and innocent.

"Really? That's not fair. You know I can't say no to your puppy dog eyes. . . . Okay, fine Leah heard the rattling of Lucy's bedside table draw. "Let's think."

"Write down cupcakes."

Leah mentally noted that Micah had a one-track mind: cupcakes.

"I *know*. . . . What time is it anyway? You woke me up to show me the note. Which you did *not* need me to read."

"I know. *But* I wanted you to know what it said, too." Leah could hear the grin in his voice. "I woke up at 5:40 and played in my room. It's 6:40 now. At least I waited an hour for you before I pulled it out of the frame and tore it open."

"Mi-*cah*! It's too early for me. Let's do this later."

"You said we could do it now."

"That's because I didn't know how early it is!"

"If we wait much longer, Mommy will be up, and I want to do it with you."

"Brothers," mumbled Lucy under her breath. "I mean, how nice."

Leah held in a laugh.

"Cupcakes."

"I got it already. What else?"

"I think we should play games."

"What kind of games?"

"I got it. Reindeer games."

Leah just knew Lucy was rolling her eyes. "'kay," she sighed.

"Lucy, how *do* we play reindeer games?" asked Micah. "I mean, what kinds of games do they play?"

Lucy yawned. "It's just a part of the song, bubby. 'They wouldn't let poor Rudolph play in any reindeer games.' Probably just tag or something."

"I don't think that's right."

"Micah . . ." Lucy trailed off.

"Will you Google it? Can we look it up on your tablet?"

"Fine." More scuffling. "I can't believe I'm Googling reindeer games," she mumbled.

Leah heard movement on the bed and assumed Micah was getting closer, wanting a better look at the tablet.

"Here's one, bubba. What if we have Mama buy

some balloons and pantyhose and then have everyone *make* antlers by stuffing the balloons in the pantyhose?"

"What are pantyhose? That sounds gross. *Pantyhose?!*"

"It is a kind of funny name. Pantyhose are like tights, like what I wear for dance? But they're not as thick. Grown-ups are usually the ones who wear them. Grown-up *women*, I mean. Yippee."

Leah bit her lip to keep from laughing out loud. *I feel the same way, Lucy.*

Lucy's sarcasm made Micah giggle. "That sounds like a fun game, even if that's a weird name."

"Okay, I'll add it to the list so Mama can buy what we need."

"Sissy?"

"Yeah, bubba?"

"Do you think some of our friends would sign the Christmas cards?"

"That's a *great* idea, bubba! Yes! I'll put that down on our list. Anything else?"

"Do you think they'll bring birthday presents?"

"I don't think so, since it would be hard to actually give them to Jesus in person. Maybe we could ask them to bring a new toy for us to give to Toys for Tots. Then we can donate those."

"What's Toys for Tots again?" asked Micah.

"It's a collection that some people do. They collect

toys to give to kids who might not get very much for Christmas otherwise."

"I like that idea. Thanks, Lucy."

"No problem. I'll write that down, too. Can I go back to sleep now?"

"But we need more—"

"This is a good start, Micah," interrupted Lucy. "But I'm so tired. We can finish later, okay?"

"Okay." He hopped off the bed and Leah hurried off before Micah ran back to his room.

December 17

Dear Lucy and Micah,

    I love your ideas for the birthday party. I think having it on the nineteenth is a great idea, and I've let our friends know when, where, and to please bring unwrapped toys for Toys for Tots. What a great idea! I also like that you are planning to ask them to sign some cards for the rescue mission. You were full of good ideas. Today, we are delivering brittle to Uncle JJ and to Miss Ida. I know seeing you two will brighten her day.

    Love,

Mama

"Mommy?"

"Yes, Micah?"

"Who's Miss Ida again?"

"Your school bus driver."

Micah thought for a moment. "I thought that was Mr. Hank."

"No, bubba," said Lucy. "It's Miss Ida. Well," she corrected herself, "it's Mr. Hank right now, but Miss Ida was our bus driver last year. And the year before and the year before and, you know. She's out right now because she had to have surgery. Mr. Hank is just a sub."

"Oh. I forgot."

Leah smiled at her son. "Miss Ida will be back after Christmas break. I know she misses her kids, so it will be nice for you to see her this afternoon."

"How do you know where she lives?" asked Lucy.

"I lived a couple of houses down from her before I married Daddy." Leah's voice quieted to a conspiratorial whisper. "She used to have her bus at her house overnight. The schools don't let anyone do that anymore."

"She was your *neighbor*?" asked Micah, awestruck. "Did she ever let you get on the bus and play with the doors?"

"Micah!" exclaimed Lucy. "Of course not! Don't be silly."

Micah's face dropped, but Leah broke in. "Actually, she did let me do it *once*. It's pretty fun."

"So cool." Micah looked at the boxes of brittle. "Do we have some for Mr. Hank, too?"

The tender heart of her nine-year-old brought a smile to Leah's face. "Yes, we have enough for him, too. I think he'll be pleased that you thought of him."

"I'm gonna make him a card!"

Micah ran out of the room, and Lucy sat next to Leah. As she rested her head on Leah's shoulder, Leah slipped her arm around the tween.

"Mama?"

"Yes, Lucy-girl?" Leah rested her cheek on Lucy's head.

"I love you."

"I love you, too, Miss."

"I miss Daddy."

"Me, too."

"I'm glad we made his favorite brittle, but do you think he'd be happy we're giving it away?"

"Well," Leah began carefully, "I think he would be happy we made it and that we were thinking about him and talking about him while we did. I think that if he was here, he'd not *want* to share his *favorite*, but I think he'd still be so excited for us to share it with other people."

"I think so, too," agreed Lucy. "Do you think he'd decorate the boxes before we gave them away?"

Leah warmed at the question, recalling how Jacob would doodle on everything. *It makes it more personal*, he'd say. "I can guarantee he would."

They sat in the silence of the moment, mother and daughter lost in their memories.

"Mama?"

"Yeah?"

"Can I decorate the boxes? I can draw something, if that's okay."

"I think you're on the right track, sweetheart. Go for it."

Lucy grabbed the boxes and headed to her art table. She paused at the door, turning to face Leah. "Will you teach me to make brittle? Maybe I can make some friends using brittle when I'm older."

"Certainly. But remember, it'll break the ice, but it's up to you to build the friendship."

December 18

Dear Lucy and Micah,

We've delivered cookies, donuts, brittle, brownies, and chicken to others this month. Today, we'll open our home to others and feed them here. I want you each to invite someone over for Daddy's favorite meal. You should choose someone who lives alone to have dinner with tonight. You'll help me make dinner, too.

Love,
Mama

"MAMA! DO WE *HAVE* TO have shepherd's pie for dinner?" Lucy's face was full of disgust. "I mean, really?!"

"What?" yelled Micah. "I hate shepherd's pie."

Leah reassured her children. "No, we're not making shepherd's pie."

"I thought we were making Daddy's favorite?" Lucy's face twisted in confusion.

"Well, my loves, Daddy *did* like shepherd's pie, but it wasn't his favorite. His favorite was chicken fajitas with mango pineapple salsa."

"Oh." Micah nodded. "I'll eat those."

"Me, too."

"Shepherd's pie was his favorite when he was a kid, and he really wanted you to try it. He hoped you'd love it, too, but it's okay that you don't."

Lucy shook her head and stuck out her tongue. "Good thing, because blech."

"Who should we invite?" wondered Leah.

"What about Pastor Dale? Miss Peggy died so he doesn't have anyone at home now."

"Good idea, Micah. I like that."

"What about Miss Marge? Her kids live far away, so she's in her big house all by herself."

"Great choice, Lucy."

"I'll call them later. For now, you two can cut some peppers and onions. I'll cut some chicken and marinade it."

"Onions? Are they gonna make me cry?"

"I don't know, sis, they might." Leah reached into the cabinet and pulled out three cutting boards. "Did you know that this meal is the first thing your daddy ever made for me?"

Micah's chocolate brown eyes stared up at her. His appearance was so much like his daddy that it took her breath away. She slid a finger across her cheek, catching a tear as it fell from her eye.

"Maybe that's why I like it so much," said Lucy, slipping her arm around Leah. "I think this is my favorite thing that Daddy made. I'm glad we're sharing it for dinner tonight."

"It is pretty yummy." Leah pulled the chicken out of the fridge and grabbed her cutting board. She started slicing the chicken breast and dropping it into a Ziploc gallon bag.

Lucy watched for a moment. She cocked her head to the side as she watched Leah methodically prep the chicken. "Why do you put it in the bag?"

"I could put it in a bowl, but I'm going for easy cleanup today. We have some errands to run after we're done getting everything ready for dinner. We need to get supplies for the birthday party tomorrow, as well as a few other things."

Leah finished cutting the chicken, added seasonings, and washed her hands.

"Could you get me the salsa from the fridge?" She zipped the bag and shook it, distributing the seasonings to coat the chicken. "There we go."

Lucy handed her the jar of salsa. "This is Daddy's secret salsa?"

Leah snickered. "Yup. He hated making salsa, so this is the brand he used. It tastes good, so we're gonna go with it."

"Oh, Daddy." Lucy rolled her eyes and shrugged. "At least it'll be easy for me to remember."

December 19

Dear Lucy and Micah,

Pastor Dale and Miss Marge seemed to enjoy dinner last night. Thank you for helping me make it and for inviting them. You had an awesome idea to ask them to sign some cards for the rescue mission, too.

It's birthday party day! Before your friends arrive, please clean your rooms and help me get the living room ready for everyone.

Love,

Mama

"I HAVE THE CARD-SIGNING station at the island in the kitchen, Mama." Lucy, a bounce in her step, waved her hands around as she explained to Leah the decision to put it there. "I thought, this way, the dining table is still available for games and crafts. And cards won't get lost like if we tried to sign them in the living room without a table."

"Good thinking, Lucy-girl." Leah pulled Lucy into a side hug. "I'm so proud of both of you. You put a lot of thought into what your friends would like and what would be special about it."

Lucy grabbed Leah's hand and pulled her into the bathroom, shutting the door behind her. "I wish I could say that I came up with it all, but it was really Micah. He had the idea for the baby Jesus cupcakes that he saw you make last year. He came up with the idea of decorating little trees. The only thing I did was say we should have the cards out for other kids to sign." She paused. "I guess I did mention Toys for Tots, too, but once I mentioned it, he agreed that it would be good."

"Micah notices everything, doesn't he?"

Lucy nodded. "He hears everything, too, so be careful what you say around him."

Leah laughed. "I know. He's like a little sponge, absorbing everything."

"You laugh, Mama, but I think you're right." She stilled as she listened at the door. "I think it's safe for us to go out. Don't tell him I told you, 'kay? He'll tease me forever."

"We'll see. Let's get out there. I need to get the tree decorating station set up in the dining room while you two work on your reindeer games, whatever those are." She opened the door and walked toward the living room.

Lucy smiled. "You'll see."

Micah had insisted on letting his friends decorate their own trees to take home and display in their rooms. It had taken some finagling on Leah's part, but she'd finally convinced him to forgo real Christmas trees and offer two kinds of trees instead: felt ones that kids could glue things onto and ones on canvas. She'd made some tree outlines and ironed them on to some small canvases for Lucy and Micah's friends to paint. She'd picked up some battery-operated LED strands that could be poked through, as well. She was as excited as Micah to see what kind of trees everyone made.

When she walked into the living room, she gasped. "Whoa." Lucy had dug out an old Happy Birthday banner to hang. There were small balloons everywhere.

"Like it, Mama?"

"Mommy, it's for our reindeer game." Micah was smiling. "I said reindeer games, and Lucy did some Googling. That's why we needed pantyhose—weird name—and balloons." Lucy stepped over the balloons and picked up a pair of pantyhose. "Everyone grabs balloons and stuffs them in here as fast as they can. When they think they have enough to make the pantyhose stand up and out, they put them on like a hat. So, they haaaaave . . . wait for it." She paused for effect. "Antlers." Another pause. "Like reindeer."

Leah put her face in her hands as giggles escaped. Tears fell as she laughed.

"It's kind of a dad joke, you know?" said Lucy. "I think Daddy would have loved it."

Leah swiped the back of her hand across her face. "I think so, too." She inhaled slowly, trying to stop laughing, and looked around. "Do you think we should make one of the canvas trees as an example for your friends?"

"Good idea," agreed Lucy. She turned and yelled, "Micah!"

Micah came running in. "What? Did some balloons pop?"

Leah smiled. "No, no popping. I was wondering if you'd like to make a Christmas tree canvas before your friends come?"

"Sure," said Micah, shrugging. He led the way to the dining room, where he snagged a canvas and some paints before sitting at the table.

"So, paint the tree, then add ornaments on it or presents under it or whatever. Don't goop the paint on, though. We want it to dry quickly." Leah sat across from him, following his movements as he painted the tree using different shades of green.

"Is this okay, Mommy?" He faced the painting toward her.

"It looks great, Micah." She gently touched the top of the tree. "Perfect amount of paint, too. Not goopy at all."

"That's a funny word: *goopy*," chuckled Micah. He turned it back around and started putting bright-colored balls on the tree. "Ornaments." He finished the tree and let it sit for a few minutes.

"Can you grab one of the strands of lights? And the paper clip?"

Micah nodded and picked up the items. "Why do we need the paper clip?"

"Once you tell me where you want the lights, we'll use the paper clip to poke a tiny hole in the canvas to poke the light through. We'll glue the control to the inside of the frame on the back of the canvas. Then voila!"

Ten minutes later, Micah turned on the lights of his Christmas tree painting. His face glowed with pride. "Thanks, Mommy. My friends are gonna love this party!"

December 20

Dear Lucy and Micah,

Your friends had so much fun yesterday! I love that you sang "Happy Birthday" and that you played reindeer games. Today, we will deliver the toys from the party to Toys for Tots.

Love,

Mama

THE TONE IN THE MINIVAN was somber as they drove home after their drop-off for Toys for Tots. Leah recognized her children's need to process what they'd learned, and she turned the upbeat Christmas music off.

Micah was the first to ask. "Is that true, Mommy? Do some kids *not* get presents for Christmas?"

Lucy, who often felt much older than twelve, answered him. "Yeah, bubba. Some kids only get one or two, or maybe even none."

"But what about Santa?"

"Bubby, Santa's not—"

"Always welcome in some homes." Leah glanced in the mirror at Lucy, who realized what she'd almost done. "Some families don't want some old guy in a red suit coming down their chimney."

"I don't either when you put it that way!" cried Lucy.

Micah laughed. "That *does* sound creepy, Mama."

Leah snickered. "You're right. I never thought of it that way." She shrugged. "Regardless, Toys for Tots helps Santa get gifts to kids who might not get something. Those Marines, as tall as they are, are kind of like elves."

"They should be wearing elf costumes when they collect the gifts." Lucy giggled. "Can you imagine them in tights and a long elf shirt? Jingly hat and pointy ears? That would be funny to see."

"Oooh!" exclaimed Micah. "Or when they deliver." He nodded his head like that was the best idea ever.

Leah's breath slowed as she listened to them continue to chatter about how the Marines were elves, as well as who else they know that might secretly be an elf. Her heart was full.

"I think Daddy was an elf."

Leah's ears perked at Micah's declaration, and she glanced in the rearview mirror.

Lucy gave him The Look—the look Leah saw on

her face too frequently. The one that said, *Are you crazy?* or *I don't believe you think that.*

Leah spoke over her shoulder, interjecting before Lucy could voice The Look. "Why do you think that?"

"He *always* got a picture of Santa putting presents under our tree." Micah gave Lucy a *duh* look.

"Yeah. And?" Lucy's tween attitude, dubbed *tween-itude* by Leah, was in full force.

"How else would he get it? Santa wouldn't let just *anyone* take his picture."

Lucy couldn't argue with his reasoning. "You know, bubba, I think you might be right. What do you think, Mama?"

Leah pondered it before answering with a smile, "I think I'm not allowed to talk about who may or may not be one of Santa's elves."

Micah's eyes widened. "Wait. Are you saying—" He paused. "Mommy? Are *you* an elf?" His jaw remained open as he thought about the implications. "If you're an elf and Daddy was an elf, does that mean I'm an elf? And Lucy is an elf?!" He looked across the minivan at his sister, her arms crossed. "She's not a very happy elf."

"I'm not an elf, Micah." Lucy pulled off her fuzzy hat and pushed her blonde hair behind her ears. "See? No pointy ears."

"I don't know, Lucy, you might have special coverings for them."

"Micah."

"What?"

"Check your own ears, bub. I promise we're not elves." Lucy shook her head.

In the driver's seat, Leah was biting her lip as she listened to the exchange. When Micah asked her again if she was an elf, she gave the same answer as before: "I'm not allowed to talk about who may or may not be one of Santa's elves."

Micah smirked. "I know what that means, Mama. And Lucy?" He faced his sister next to him. "You can't convince me otherwise."

December 21

Dear Lucy and Micah,

It snowed last night! Today, we're going to use Daddy's snowblower to take care of Miss Carol's and Mr. Johnson's sidewalks for them. Daddy always helped Miss Carol after her husband passed, and Mr. Johnson usually uses a shovel. Then we'll come home, make snow angels, and have hot chocolate.

Love,
Mama

THEIR FACES WERE FLUSHED AS they stripped out of their wet clothes. "Go grab some blankets, and I'll make the hot chocolate." Leah hurried to the kitchen and put some milk on the stove to heat.

"That was. So. Much. Fun!" Micah's eyes shone with joy as Leah returned to the living room.

"Yes!" agreed Lucy. She paused. "I wish Daddy was here to do it with us."

Leah knelt beside them and wrapped her arms around them. "Me, too, sweetheart."

"He loved to make snow angels." Lucy sobbed in her mom's shoulder.

"No, he didn't," cried Micah.

"Yes, he did!"

"No, he didn't. He liked for *us* to make snow angels." Micah wrapped his blanket tight around him.

"He helped us make snowmen," pouted Lucy.

"And he threw snowballs at us," added Micah. "But not hard."

Lucy sunk into a chair. "I miss him."

"Me, too."

"Me, three." Leah hugged Lucy and Micah, grateful her children were sharing. "What's your favorite Christmastime memory with Daddy?"

"I loved when we drove around and looked at the lights on everyone's house." Lucy sighed. "That was the only time he'd *buy* us hot chocolate. We'd sip on it."

"Oh, yeah! We'd get it right before we went to see the Nelson family lights," added Micah. "Remember?"

Leah nodded. "I do. You usually drank all of your hot chocolate while we were watching their light and music show, so we'd stop and get another after we left their house."

"I always loved doing that." Lucy rubbed her cheek

with her blanket, wiping away a tear. "Could we do that tonight?"

"Yeah, we can. We'll go right after dinner."

"Thanks, Mama."

"Of course, sweetheart." Leah watched Micah, squirming on the couch. "What about you, bubba? What's one of your favorite Christmastime memories?"

"It's not just a *Christmas* memory, but it happened then, too." He smiled. "Sitting on his lap for family movie night until he fell asleep during the movie."

Leah and Lucy broke into laughter, recalling all the times Jacob would kick the recliner back and have Micah crawl up on his lap, only to fall asleep a few minutes into the movie. Christmas movies seemed to make it happen even faster. After Jacob fell asleep, Micah would climb down and put a blanket over him, even in the summer.

"I think the only time Daddy didn't fall asleep during the movie was if we were watching *A Christmas Story*. And even then, he still did sometimes." Lucy wiped more tears. "And if it was a musical? Forget about it! He'd be asleep before the opening scene was over."

Leah nodded, picturing Jacob in the chair Lucy was perched on. She offered the kids a small smile. "Good memories, you two. One of my favorites is when we'd stay up and wrap presents one night after you went to bed." She fingered the dainty chain around her neck, pulling out the ring that was on it. "While we wrapped, we'd talk about all we wanted for our family for the coming year. Our hopes. Our dreams for each of you and each other." She blinked back tears and stood. "I need to check on the milk for your hot chocolate ."

She hurried to the kitchen and stirred the milk, glad she had turned it on very low. She turned the heat up as tears streamed down her face. She gasped as two sets of arms slipped around her. Lucy lay her head on Leah's shoulder as Micah rested his head against Leah's back. Leah closed her eyes, silently thanking God for the gift of her children .

December 22

"STOP! I CAN CARRY IT!" Micah turned and glared at Lucy, who was trying to take a box out of his hands.

"Mama, Micah won't let me carry the box."

"Lucy, there's a box for each of us. Grab one of the others." They were standing at the back of the minivan, unloading their cards and candy canes to take inside.

"But I wanted this one," whined Lucy.

Leah stared at her for a moment before taking a deep breath. "Why this one?"

Lucy bit her lip and looked down. "Because it's smaller than the others."

"Seriously?" asked Micah. He looked at the other boxes. "I thought they were all the same."

"Actually," began Lucy, "the boxes are pretty close, but this one has fewer cards in it, so it isn't as heavy as the other two."

"Oh, okay." Micah handed the box to Lucy and picked up a different box. "Oh, man! You're right. This one is a lot heavier!" He laughed. "Let's go!"

"Do you need me to get it, Micah?" offered Leah.

"Nope. I'm good."

"If Daddy was here, we wouldn't have to carry any of the dumb boxes." Lucy sniffled.

Leah took the box from Lucy's hands and set it down before wrapping her arms around her daughter. "I miss him, too."

Lucy sobbed into Leah's shoulder. "Do you think Daddy would be happy we're doing this?"

"I do."

"Okay." Lucy pulled away from the hug and wiped her arm across her face. "Okay. I'm ready."

"Good!" came Micah's response. "Because this box is getting heavy!"

They walked inside, and Leah poked her head into the office. "Hi. We called about bringing Christmas cards for everyone. I'm looking for Tammi?"

The woman behind the desk brightened. "I'm Tammi. You must be Leah." She grinned as Lucy and Micah came through the doorway. "And this must be Micah and Lucy. This is so kind of you. Not many people think of bringing us cards to give each person who stays here."

Lucy's brow furrowed as she absorbed that information. "They stay here? I thought they just came here for a meal or to stay warm?"

"Some do," agreed Tammi, "but did you see those small buildings on your way in?" When Lucy and Micah nodded, she continued. "Those are called tiny shelters, and people stay in them. They sleep there. They keep their things in there. They have privacy there."

The trio walked into the office, and Tammi motioned for them to have a seat. Each of them sat with their box in their lap.

"They aren't very big buildings. Do they have bathrooms in them?" Leave it to Micah to check on bathroom status.

"No, there's no running water in those buildings, but they come in here for meals, showers, laundry, and bathroom needs."

"This is for people who don't have a place to live?" asked Lucy, confused. "How long do they live here?"

"They can stay for three months, sometimes six. It depends on what they're doing to change their situation. We hope to help them make a way to find housing apart from us."

Lucy contemplated this. Leah's thoughts were whirling, too. "I didn't realize that so much was happening here. You actively care for the least of these. Maybe I can come back after the new year and volunteer in some way."

"That would be wonderful! All three of you could, if you'd like. We have opportunities for service that nearly any age or ability could do." Tammi waved her arm toward the dining room outside her office door. "It takes a lot to do all we do, and we love our volunteers." She motioned to a table along the wall of her office. "You can leave the boxes there. We'll pass them out either tonight at dinner or tomorrow at lunch. Thank you again for the cards." She stood and walked to the door. "I have an appointment in just a few minutes, or I'd love to chat more. Please, call me when you're ready to volunteer." She shook their hands as they left the office.

They were quiet on the walk back to their minivan. Only when they were driving away did anyone speak. "Mama?" asked Lucy. "I'd like to volunteer, too, if that's okay."

Leah's heart swelled. "I think that's more than okay."

December 23

Dear Lucy and Micah,

It is <u>really</u> cold outside! The Salvation Army bellringers are still out in full force, so we are going to take some hot chocolate, coffee, and hot tea around to the ones we see this morning.

Love,

Mama

"GINA!" LEAH GREETED THE BELLRINGER with a hug as her children huddled just inside the store entrance, avoiding the wind and holding a drink carrier. "I didn't know you were doing this. How did I not know this?"

Gina was bundled up with a scarf, earmuffs, boots, and a thick winter coat. Her cheeks and nose were flushed from the cold. She smiled as a couple walked past and dropped some bills into her bucket. "Thank you and Merry Christmas!" she called after them. She turned to Leah, who pulled on her hood and tucked her hands in her pockets. "I was trying to think of something I could do that would be helpful in addition to serving Christmas dinner at a shelter. This felt like an opportunity that would help a lot of people, but not many would want to do. I mean, I stand outside in the cold for a few hours at a time. No skiing, ice skating, or snowball fights involved. I haven't really talked about it much, so you haven't really missed anything."

"That's awesome. Do you enjoy it?"

"It's been a lot of fun." She knelt to talk to a child who walked up. "Hi! Merry Christmas and thank you for giving!" She offered a high five after the little boy put the money in the bucket. He responded before running back to his dad at the store entrance. "I love when kids come up to give."

"It's a great thing to see," agreed Leah. She eyed the busy shoppers coming and going. "Harringtons' is busy today."

"Two days before Christmas means last-minute shopping." Gina shrugged and reached for Leah's arm and gave a small squeeze. "How are you doing?"

Tears welled up and threatened to spill over as Leah's throat thickened. She shrugged. "I'm doing. I cry after the kids go to bed or in the shower."

Gina had to lean in to hear her. "Leah, it's okay to let them see you cry."

"Oh, I know." She waved her hand. "I cry with them

when they're already missing him, but I don't want to add it if they're having a good day." She dropped her voice to a whisper. "Micah notices *everything*. He *feels* everything. If I tear up, he will, too, simply because he's sad that I'm sad. It's so sweet, but it's a lot for a nine-year-old to feel."

As Gina pulled Leah in for a hug, she whispered, "God is holding you in His hands. He has plans for you. For Micah. For Lucy. Lean on Him."

Leah nodded as she stepped back. "I'm leaning on Him so hard, Gina. I can't even explain. One day, I'll tell you the story of all the ways God has provided for us since Jacob died. I mean, the people God has used to love us? The people He has prompted to offer time or talent or even money to sustain us while I waited for everything to settle? I am humbled and beyond grateful for all of the help given to us by everyone."

"I can't wait to hear it." She rang the bell as people walked past. "We need to plan a lunch date soon."

Leah wiped the tears away from her eyes and shook her head. "Yes, we do. Maybe after Christmas break is over? That way the kids are in school."

"That would be perfect. When do they go back?"

"January fourth." Leah pulled her phone from her coat pocket.

"Could we tentatively plan for the sixth? I'll have to check my calendar, but I'm pretty sure I'm open that day."

Leah swiped through the calendar app on her phone. "I can do that. I'm open all day."

"Put me in. I'll text you when I get home this evening to confirm a time and place."

"Sounds great." She closed the app and slid her phone back in her pocket. "Okay. We came bearing a gift for the bellringer, which just so happens to be you, soooo . . ." She motioned to Lucy and Micah to bring the drink carriers. "I know you've always loved coffee, but we also have hot chocolate and hot tea."

"Oh! How kind of you! A hot drink is perfect today." Gina scrunched her nose as she decided. "How about a hot chocolate today?"

Leah lifted one out of the carrier and passed it to Gina. "Enjoy! And stay warm today."

"Thank you so much." Gina smiled at Lucy and Micah. "I will."

"Bye, Miss Gina!" They turned and Leah took the carriers as her children skipped down the sidewalk.

"I love giving out hot chocolate!" shouted Lucy.

"Me, too!" echoed Micah .

December 24

Dear Lucy and Micah,

It's Christmas Eve. Can you believe it?! Today, I would like for you to each make two coupon books. One for your sibling and one for someone else you would like to help over the next year. Think carefully.

Love,

Mama

LEAH WALKED INTO THE KITCHEN and peered at the two little blonde heads bent close together over the kitchen table.

"Shh! She'll hear you!"

"No! She'll hear you!"

"I hear both of you." Leah grinned as both kids looked at her and quickly turned back around to cover what they were working on.

"Whatcha doin'?"

"Something." Tweenitude.

"Do I need to investigate?"

"No, Mama." The tone was sharp, and Lucy realized it immediately. She got up and hugged Leah. "Sorry, Mama. I mean, no, we don't want you to investigate. We got our note for today, and we're working on it. That's all." She slipped back into her seat at the table.

"Oh, I see." Leah busied herself with making coffee. "Did you decide who else you're making coupons for?"

"Yep," came Micah's quick response.

"Do you need my help?"

"Nope." Lucy this time.

"You mean I get to have a lazy day?"

Micah laughed, "Well, if you *want* to, but it *is* Christmas Eve."

"Wait, it's Christmas Eve?!" gasped Leah.

Lucy and Micah looked at her and shook their heads. "You knew that already," said Micah. They turned back to their project.

Leah chuckled. She wondered what they were writing on their coupons. She cozied into her recliner and opened her Advent devotional to read while she waited for them. She loved slow-to-start days.

Twenty minutes later, they raced into the living room. "We're done!"

"That was fast."

"We worked on it a lot before you found us in the

kitchen," shrugged Lucy. "We were super quiet this morning." Micah nodded his agreement.

"Thank you for that."

"No problem." Micah's matter-of-fact nature never failed to make Leah smile.

"Anyway, Mama, we made a coupon book for Miss Dolores at church. Micah said he'd shovel her snow, rake her leaves, and mow her grass twice this year. Two times each thing."

Micah gave his cheesiest grin.

"She's asked if I might want to learn to knit, so I'm going to take knitting lessons from her," Lucy said.

Leah raised an eyebrow.

"I think she just wants a visitor, but this way she has a reason for the visit and doesn't think it's pity."

Now Leah raised both eyebrows.

"It's *not* pity. So, I don't want her to think it is."

"That's great, anything else?"

"I also put a batch of peanut butter cookies on a coupon for her. I know she loves books, but she has a hard time reading because of her dyslexia, so I also put that I'd read three books to her this year. I just hope she doesn't pick *War and Peace*."

"Those are so great, you two." She pulled them in for a family hug. "I'm so proud of you and what you came up with for her."

Micah beamed.

"We have one more," started Lucy.

"And we picked *you*!" Micah jumped as he said it.

"Oh." Leah was speechless.

"Mama, you're always looking out for other people. Like helping Mr. Dustin and Miss Josie after baby Graham was born. I know you're going over there again in a couple of days. You take meals to people all the time, even when it's not part of our kindness challenge. You take Miss Dolores to her doctors' appointments. You serve in the nursery at church. You have lunch with Miss Carol once a week while we're at school."

"How did you—"

"She told us. When we took cookies that day. I think she thought we knew." Lucy squeezed onto the recliner with Leah, and Micah climbed onto Leah's lap. "You do a lot of things to help, and you think no one sees. We want you to know that we do. This year, especially. I'm almost a teenager, Mama. I notice things."

Leah wiped a tear from her cheek. "I guess you do. You're growing up way too fast."

Lucy waved the comment away. "Anyway, we've made a coupon book for you. Micah wants to start taking care of the floors. He will vacuum, sweep, Swiffer, whatever. Three times a week, all year."

"That's a lot."

Micah raised one shoulder. "Eh, I know. It's okay."

Lucy continued, "I am going to dust every weekend. I'm also going to do my own laundry. I know how, but if I need help, I'll ask."

Micah turned and put his forehead against Leah's. "I'm going to do my own laundry, too." He leaned back. "I might need some help, though."

Leah giggled. "Okay."

"We are both going to wash our own hot chocolate mugs every time we make it." Lucy closed her eyes. "I know it's not a big thing, but we use a *lot* of mugs for hot chocolate."

Leah could feel the sting of her tears before they slid down her cheeks. "These are perfect. Thank you. You two are so awesome. I have the best kids."

December 25

Dear Lucy and Micah,

It's the last day we celebrate this month, although I do hope you find kind things to do for people all year round. Today, we head to the movies, as usual on this day. This time, however, I would like for you to watch the people behind us while we wait in line. Each of you should pick one person who looks like they came alone, and we will pay for their ticket. Hopefully they'll feel loved today. I'm so proud of both of you, and I love you very much.

Love,
Mama

LUCY AND MICAH BOUNCED ON their toes as they waited in line, looking behind them for someone to give free tickets. Leah peered at the matinee to see what was playing. They usually saw the new family movie, but the theater had started something new this year and were showing a different "oldie" every day.

"Hey, kids." She waved her hand behind her to get their attention while she focused on the movies that were playing. "Guys?" She reached back again but didn't find them. "Lucy? Micah?" She turned around and gasped. Her hand went to her chest, and she rubbed the necklace she was wearing, which held Jacob's wedding ring .

"Mama! Look who I found!" Lucy held tight to Miss Carol's hand, pulling her along.

"Hi, Carol." Leah reached for the older woman and embraced her. When they stepped back, Leah noticed the tears in her eyes and nodded in understanding. She squeezed her hand. "Please let us pay for your ticket today."

"Hey, Mommy! I found Pastor Dale!" Micah came running to her, then stopped to turn around and run back to the retired minister. "Come on," he stage-whispered. "It's okay, really!"

As they approached, Leah reached out and gave Dale a hug. "It's nice to see you today."

"Thank you, it's nice to see you three, too." He studied the line he had surpassed. "I just needed to be around people today."

"No need to explain, my friend." Leah indicated the woman next to her. "This is my neighbor and friend, Carol. Carol, this is my friend, Dale."

The two shook hands before returning their gaze to Leah. "Do you know what you want to see?" asked Leah. "We usually do the newest family movie, but I saw the 'oldie' they're offering. It was Jacob's favorite, so I thought we might watch it instead." She turned to the kids, who had high-fived each other. "I take it that's okay?"

"Yes!" they exclaimed.

Carol smiled sadly. "That was my Robert's favorite, too." Her head dropped. "It's the reason I came today. It's kind of like he's here with me."

"It's not really my favorite," said Dale, "but Jacob introduced me to it a few years ago. I could see it again."

"You don't have to see that. We'll still pay for your ticket."

"I didn't have a definite plan for what I was going to see. Like I said, I just needed to be around people today."

"Will you sit with us?" asked Micah. Leah observed his interaction with Dale, noting to herself that a month ago, he would barely talk to anyone besides her.

"Certainly, young Micah." Dale smiled at the boy beside him. "I'll even tell you, 'You'll shoot your eye out, kid!' if you want."

The others laughed. Lucy continued to hold Miss Carol's hand, like she was afraid her neighbor would scurry away from them if she let go.

Leah paid for their tickets, and they started toward

the usher taking the tickets. She slowed and considered the group chattering. *An odd mix*, she thought, *but brought together in our grief.* She thought of Jacob, wishing again that he was still with them, saddened that he'd no longer be with them for special occasions—or even every day. It was in the everyday things that she missed him most.

"Mama?" Leah blinked when she felt Lucy's hand in hers. "Mama?"

"Yes, my little love?"

Lucy hugged her mom and looked up at her. "I know Daddy isn't here anymore, but this month, with the things you had us do? Things that were his favorite, things he liked to do? It felt like God gave us just what we needed to feel like Daddy was here. It was kind of like he was with us again, home for the holidays, even though he wasn't, you know?"

Leah wrapped her arms around her daughter and kissed the top of her head. "Yeah," she whispered. "I do."

Your Kindness Challenge

If you would like to do your own kindness challenge but aren't sure where to start, here are some ideas. Feel free to tweak them to fit your own lifestyle, family favorites, and traditions, of course!

- Make cookies for someone else.
- Shovel a neighbor's sidewalk (or sweep, if it's not snowy).
- Write an encouraging note to give to someone you see at the store.
- Ask an older loved one to talk about their childhood.
- Thank your cashier by name.
- Pick up trash at a local park.
- Leave coins in a vending machine.
- Tell a family member one of your favorite memories with them.
- Hold the door for someone else.

- Donate toys, clothes, diapers, or food.
- Make and send a card for someone you love.
- Write a jar of compliments for your family.
- Try not to complain about anything today.
- Let someone go in front of you in line.
- Learn a new joke to tell someone.
- Read to someone.
- Slip a gift card into a package of diapers at the store.
- Babysit for a friend who needs a break.
- Buy a coffee for the person behind you.
- Leave a generous tip for your favorite server.
- Smile at everyone you see today.

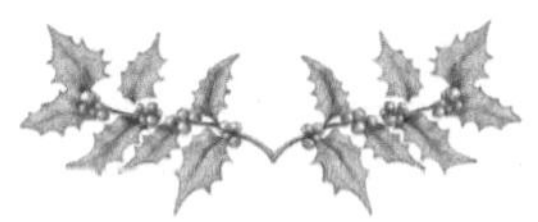

Recipes

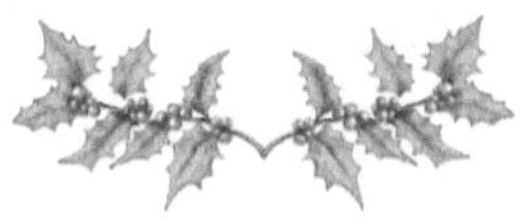

Sue's Melt-in-Your-Mouth Sugar Cookies

This recipe comes from a sweet friend I met when I was living in Illinois. Sue Roper has a heart for missions, and these cookies were often a prize on Missions night at church, when she would ask a missions-related question. Funnily enough, the one time I knew the answer, the prize was fudge (also yummy). As a consolation before I moved to Washington, she shared the recipe with me. The cookies are super soft and light. The buttercream frosting recipe was included when she passed me the cookie recipe.

Ingredients
1 cup butter
1 cup vegetable oil
1 cup powdered sugar
1 cup sugar + more for rolling
2 eggs
1 tablespoon vanilla
1 teaspoon baking soda
5 cups flour
1 teaspoon cream of tartar
1 teaspoon salt

Directions
Preheat the oven to 375°F.

Cream butter, vegetable oil, and sugars together. Blend in eggs and vanilla.

Add dry ingredients to the wet mixture and mix well.

Form dough into balls about the size of walnuts, roll in sugar, and place on ungreased cookie sheet. Flatten the balls slightly and bake for 10 minutes.

Remove immediately and let cool.

Cookies can be frosted (or dipped in cinnamon & sugar mix prior to baking). These cookies are not easy to make into cut-outs because the dough is so soft.

Buttercream Frosting

Ingredients
1/3 cup butter
3 cups powdered sugar
1½ teaspoon vanilla
2–3 tablespoons milk

Directions
Cream the butter and slowly add the powdered sugar and vanilla. Add the milk in small increments until the frosting reaches the consistency you want. Remember to make the frosting fairly stiff if you are adding food coloring, unless using the gel coloring.

Aunt Dot's Cut-Out
Sugar Cookies

This recipe is for the Christmas sugar cookies I grew up having. It is my Aunt Dot's recipe, and she generously shared it with me. Aunt Dot was a busy ER nurse for many years, but despite the hectic schedule, she never failed to spend time with my grandparents, her siblings, and her nieces and nephews. Commitment to family (chosen or not) is the lesson I've learned best from her.

Ingredients
¾ cup shortening*
1 cup sugar
2 eggs
1 teaspoon vanilla or ½ teaspoon lemon extract
2½ cups all-purpose flour
1 teaspoon baking powder
1 teaspoon salt

Directions
Preheat oven to 375°F.

Mix thoroughly the shortening, sugar, eggs, and extract. Blend in flour, baking powder, and salt. Cover and chill at least 1 hour.

**You can use part softened butter/part softened margarine.*

Roll dough 1/8-inch thick on floured board and cut out with cookie cutters. Place on an ungreased baking sheet.

Bake 6 to 8 minutes (longer if cookies are thicker). When the edges brown, they're done!

Use buttercream frosting or royal icing to decorate.

Maple Bacon Pecan Brittle

Several years ago, I tried my hand at candy-making. It's one of the things I love to gift. Randee wanted me to try my hand at maple bacon pecan brittle, and after trying a few different recipes, I tweaked a few into one, which is what you'll find here.

Ingredients
2 cups granulated sugar
½ cup light corn syrup
½ cup maple syrup
1/2 cup water
1 cup cooked bacon, chopped or crumbled (8–10 raw thick-cut strips)
2 cups whole (shelled) pecans
2 teaspoon baking soda
1 teaspoon vanilla extract

Directions
Line a baking sheet with a silicone mat, parchment paper, or grease liberally with butter.

Mix the sugar, corn syrup, maple syrup, and water together in a pot. Cook over medium heat until the sugar has dissolved. Place a candy thermometer on the side of your pot and continue cooking until your mixture reaches 255°F.

Add the bacon, stirring well. Turn up the heat to medium high, stirring continuously.

When the candy thermometer reaches 265°F, add the pecans and stir thoroughly. After adding the pecans, the mixture will start getting thick and sticky. Continue cooking and stirring.

When your thermometer hits 300°F, turn off your stove and immediately remove your pot from the heat. Add the baking soda and vanilla extract right away, stirring well to make sure they are incorporated thoroughly.

Quickly pour your mixture on your prepared pan in a zigzag pattern to help it spread evenly. Spread with a spatula if necessary.

Immediately after spreading, move your pan into the refrigerator or freezer to keep the air bubbles, which lets your candy have a light, airy texture. After it cools, break it into pieces and store in an airtight container.

Resources

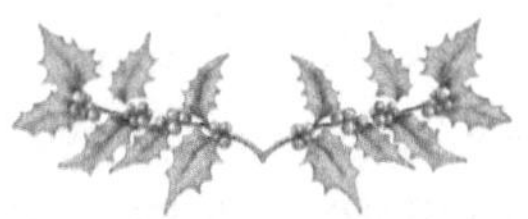

Resources for
Widowed Parents

Camps & Retreats

Camp Kangaroo, part of the Seasons Hospice Foundation, is a free bereavement camp for all children who have recently lost a loved one. https://seasonsfoundation. org/Camp-Kangaroo/

Experience Camps offers a one week camp for children who are grieving the loss of a parent, sibling, or primary caregiver. https://experiencecamps.org/camp They also offer a weekend family camp. https://experiencecamps.org/family-camp For parents, they offer an adult retreat. https://experiencecamps.org/our-programs/adult-retreat

Camp Erin seeks to help families find joy and hope in the midst of grief. https://elunanetwork.org/eluna-camps/camp-erin/

Refuge Widowers is a faith-based organization that offers retreats for men who've lost their spouse and are raising children. https://www.refugewidowers.com/retreats

Never Alone Widows is a faith-based organization for women. They aim to reach, restore, connect, and support women who've lost their spouse. They offer conferences and retreats. https://www.neveralonewidows.com/makeroom

Soaring Spirits offers "Camp Widow" https://campwidow.org/

Books
For Adults:
The Empty Chair: Handling Grief on Holidays and Special Occasions, by Susan J. Zonnebelt-Smeenge R.N. Ed.D and Robert C. De Vries

Grief Workbook For Widowed Dads: A Gentle Guided Journal to Reflect, Remember, and Rebuild After Loss, by Janina Bohm

Surviving the Holidays: Grief Survival Guide – A Practical, Faith-Based Resource for Navigating the Holiday Season After the Death of a Loved One, Featuring Biblical Encouragement, Coping Strategies, and Emotional Support from GriefShare, by The Church Initiative

Widowed Parents Unite: 52 Tips to Get Through the First Year, from One Widowed Parent to Another, by Jenny Lisk

Widowed Walk: Experiencing God After the Loss of a Spouse, by Gary Roe

The Widowed Dad's Survival Guide: A Practical Guide for Widowed Fathers, by John Fitzsimons

The Widow's Journal: Questions to Guide You through Grief and Life Planning after the Loss of a Partner, by Carrie P. Freeman, Ph.D.

For Kids:
Everywhere, Still: A Book about Loss, Grief, and the Way Love Continues, by M.H. Clark

Hi, I'm Grief, by Calle Walsha

Ida, Always, by Caron Levis

The Invisible String, by Patrice Karst

Just Like That: A Story of Hope for a Child's Grief, by Chad Current

The Memory Box: A Book About Grief, by Joanna Rowland

The Sad Dragon: A Dragon Book About Grief and Loss, by
 Steve Herman
*Something Sad Happened: Helping Children with Grief
 (Comfort for Children in Hard Times)*, by Darby A.
 Strickland
*Something Very Sad Happened: A Toddler's Guide to Under-
 standing Death*, by Bonnie Zucker
*When Someone Dies: A Children's Mindful How-To Guide
 on Grief and Loss*, by Andrea Dorn

Local and Online Communities and Organizations
 Solo Parenting Life - A group for widowed parents raising
 kids. (Facebook Community)
 Widowed Parents (Facebook Community)
 The Widowed Mom Podcast Community (Facebook
 Community)
 Never Alone Widows (local chapters) https://www.never-
 alonewidows.com/locals
 GriefShare (offers local meetings and online meetings)
 https://www.griefshare.org/
 Soaring Spirits hosts "Widowed Village" (online commu-
 nity) https://widowedvillage.org/

Other Resources
 The Widowed Mom Podcast https://www.coachingwith-
 krista.com/podcast/
 The Birdie Foundation offers a variety of resources.
 https://thebirdiefoundation.org/
 Soaring Spirits offers a Newly Widowed Packet. https://
 soaringspirits.org/programs/newly-widowed/
 GriefHaven offers a Packet of Hope for those experiencing
 fresh grief. https://griefhaven.org/resources/
 Soaring Spirits https://soaringspirits.org/

About the Author

MELISSA CATE has always been a storyteller—when she was a preschooler, her mom would record the bedtime stories Melissa would tell at night and type them up for her. After thirty years of mostly academic, devotional, or biographical writing, she jumped headfirst back into fiction in October 2023 and was a Write on the River winner in the spring of 2024. She has published four short stories in anthologies in 2025, and her first novel is planned to be published in 2026. Melissa currently lives in the Pacific Northwest with her family but is a Midwesterner through and through.

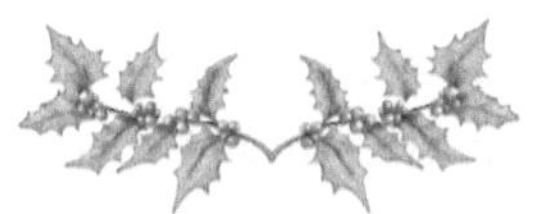

You can find Melissa on Instagram and Facebook at:
@melissacatewrites
To learn more about Melissa, visit her website at:
https://www.melissacate.com

Acknowledgments

To my sweet kids, thank you for letting me share a glimpse of our lives with others. Even though these conversations never happened, you inspired them with your humor, gentle spirits, and sweet personalities. I loved hearing your laughter over certain scenes. I think "No butts, no poop" will be your secret to laughter when the other is grumpy for now and always.

To Nicole Frail, publisher extraordinaire, thank you for believing in me and in this story. I am so grateful to have the opportunity to share it with the world. You are the best and have a great team!

To Erin Laramore, my first reader, always, I think, thank you for your encouragement for whatever I'm writing. Thank you for catching my typos and oopsies.

To Stephanie Troxler, Sarah Dempsey, and Sarah Floyd, thank you for your support. Found family is family, and I am so grateful for each of you. You've walked through my darkest days with me, and I'm glad God knew the exact friends I needed from MOPS eight years ago. Thank you for game nights, play dates, and your Godly wisdom and insight.

To Sue Roper and Dot Neutzling, the real-life women who shared their delicious sugar cookie recipes with me, thank you for your generosity in sharing these recipes with me and my readers.

To Dale Twyeffort, thank you for being more than a pastor to our family, but also a friend. You and Peggy are dear to my heart.

To Nancy McFall, who read my devotional thoughts and said, "You should write a book!" Thank you for believing I could do it.

To Paula Bashore, who handles my website for me, thank you for all of it, for everything. You're such a great friend to my family. Thank you.

To everyone who has been so supportive and helpful to me the past few months, words can never express enough the gratitude and appreciation I hold in my heart. Leah tells Gina that it's been amazing to see how God uses people to love her and her kids. That's exactly how I feel. I am incredibly thankful for every single thing—time, talent, gift cards, cash, a listening ear. It's humbling to have so many caring for me and my children. One day, I'll share all the ways I've seen God care for me through His people. For now, like Mary, I will ponder these things in my heart.

Last, but not least, to the Creator of all life, thank You, for without You, I am nothing. The joy of the Lord truly is my strength.

Also Available

Just One...

In this summer anthology, characters are denied the comfort of hiding the secrets or emotions they hold close when they are forced together as they travel to various locations.

Whether they involve the sharing of a bed or a car, or a tent on the trip of a lifetime, or something much smaller but necessary, these twelve stories are alive with tension as they highlight the challenge that is forced proximity.

Available in paperback & e-book.
Print ISBN: 978-1-965852-46-0
E-book ISBN: 978-1-965852-45-3

Welcome Home

Seven years ago, Danielle divorced Joshua without any real explanation.

Since then, she has made strides to move forward; Joshua, however, has appeared to remain mostly the same, hoping that maybe she'll someday look for him.

They meet again on a blind date and discover that the spark between them is still there. Reconciliation is on both their minds, but first, they need to resolve not only their past, as Danielle shares her reason for leaving, but also their potential future, as Joshua shares that some parts of his life have actually changed.

Can they see beyond the pain of the past and into a new future together?

Available as an ebook.
ISBN: 978-1-965852-24-8

Attic Books and Attic Ebooks
are imprints of Nicole Frail Books, LLC,
an independent ("indie") publishing
company located in Avoca, Pennsylvania.

Attic Ebooks is a digital-first imprint and is
open to submissions of various lengths,
including short stories and essays and
novellas. If the length and market allows,
longer works are considered for print with
Attic Books.

To learn more about submitting a query to
Attic Ebooks, visit www.attic-ebooks.com.

Readers!
Join the NFB Street Team for exclusive first
reads and swag from Attic & Attic Ebooks!
www.nicolefrailbooks.com/street

www.ingramcontent.com/pod-product-compliance
Lightning Source LLC
Chambersburg PA
CBHW020044310726
48970CB00007B/2401